WINTERSET

SHORT STORIES OF PIXIES, DEMONS, AND FIENDS.

BY

DENNIS MAULSBY

WINTERSET

First Edition, March 2019

ISBN: 978-1-945663-23-9

This book dedicated to

Sharon Wayne

*whose advice made
Father Donahey come alive.*

Acknowledgements

Grateful acknowledgement is made to publishers of books, periodicals, and anthologies in which these stories or earlier versions of them have appeared:

"**Night of the Pooka**" — 1st Place Award 2015 *Montezuma All-Iowa Fiction Contest*. Also published in the 2015 Fall issue of the *Mused Literary Review*. Short version published Fall of 2017 in *Lulu's Share Your Scare – Volume 1*.

"**Betty and the Demon**" — published 2017 in *Astounding Outpost* magazine (online and in anthology).

"**Two Dogs and a Pig**" — published 2018, *The Writing Piazza Press Anthology*.

"**Pixies, a Troll, and a ...**" — honorable mention in the third quarter 2018 *L. Ron Hubbard Writers of the Future Contest*.

"**The Wizard and the Queen of Demon**s" — published 2018 in the Halloween anthology *Chills Down Your Spine*, Neoleaf Press.

Other Books by Dennis Maulsby

Poetry
Near Death/Near Life

Short Stories
Freefire Zone

Author's Note:
Many thanks to Rick Hildreth, who was bitten by a pooka.

Contents

Night of the Pooka

A light glimmered in the rectory study window well past the hour when its occupants would normally be in bed. Father Ignatius Patrick Donahey sat in his favorite old wingback chair. He shivered as he turned the pages of an ancient book. Finding the reference, he paused and reached into a jacket pocket for his beloved meerschaum pipe and leather tobacco pouch. He sucked the flame of an age-scarred Zippo lighter three times into the brandy-flavored shag packed in the bowl.

The tongue-bite and honeyed smell of the smoke settled his mind and slowed his heartbeat. He reflected on the mind-boggling tales that had come from the other side of the confessional earlier in the evening. The first of the stories he could have chalked up to hysteria. However, two of the confessions meshed completely, and they came from entirely different people. The witnesses to the events, a teacher and a sheriff's deputy, were both salt of the earth members of the community.

I am much too old for this, he thought. Happily retired now, his service to the church had started over fifty years ago. Leaving a tiny backcountry Irish village at eighteen, he had progressed through the Catholic Church hierarchy from deacon to priest to Monsignor. His lifetime of employment in South American churches slowed by aging, the bishop allowed him to select from a worldwide list of parishes with light-duty positions. His natal village now only an abandoned dust heap of decaying thatch and tumbled rock walls, he chose to re-plant his rural roots in St Joseph's church in the town of Winterset, Iowa. He would spend his remaining years among a population consisting of the descendants of Irish, English, Scot, and, recently, Latino immigrants.

Donahey, while walking and biking over the surrounding country roads, had learned to love the land and admire the people, walking and biking over the surrounding country roads. Each year thousands of encircling acres grew lush with corn and soybeans — a land yet to have its fertility leached out by human exploitation. There would be time now to read all the books and think all the thoughts he wished; desires delayed and dammed up these many years by subordinating himself to the needs of his flocks. His only remaining priestly responsibility: to fill in when the local priest was sick or traveling.

So he was handling the confessional when one of the haunts of his pre-priest youth reappeared. A creature described in stories told and retold around the night fires of his childhood. His mind reconstructed the events described in the confessions.

✿

Shannon crouched in the eight-foot tall rustling September corn. Her breath came in jagged gasps. The noise of her breathing — and the pain in her side — interfered with her ability to catch the sound of her pursuers. Running through dark fields clad only in bra and panties had taken its toll. Corn leaf edges slashed and scratched exposed skin — the death of a thousand gashes. She knew from her teen years on detasseling crews that the cuts could easily become infected; exuding pus and itching like hell. Currently, this was a minor worry.

She was more scared of dashing headlong into a corn spider web. The huge webs, invisible at night, stretched across furrows. A spider, as big as a man's hand occupied the center. It would be terrifying to have one wrapped around your face, imprisoned over your eyes and mouth by its own sticky web.

She would scream, and the bad ones would find her.

Five minutes would have made all the difference. If she hadn't been working late correcting papers, the escaped convicts would have missed her. The pair threw off their pursuers by abandoning their first stolen car in the night-dark Winterset Middle School parking lot. In exchange, they took both her and her car. Purse open to retrieve keys when grabbed, Shannon had presence enough to drop her wallet without her captors noticing.

With roads and highways shut down as law enforcement officials conducted a manhunt, the two escapees holed up in her old farmhouse. Thank God, she was single; there was no husband or children to threaten.

They had not molested her the first day, their eyes and ears glued to radio and TV news, only requiring her to prepare meals. Day two, tension rose. It started with hungry looks that made her shiver. Their faces took on the grinning idiot-look of men contemplating violence. Shannon managed to keep out of their way until evening. Under cover of making a late supper, she turned the iron to its highest setting and started boiling water.

They attacked in the kitchen, pinning her against the sink. She lost shoes, blouse, and skirt in the uneven struggle. Biting one on the ear allowed her to spring free. She grabbed the iron and thrust its red-hot soleplate against neck skin. A male screeched. Shannon ran towards the backdoor. Fingers seized her thigh. She grabbed the pot handle; threw boiling water on the ankles of the second man. The screen door slammed back with the noise of a gunshot. She raced across the backyard. Plunging into the cornrows, the eight-foot tall long-leafed stalks hid her from sight.

There were ways of keeping your bearing in mature cornfields. If you went straight down a row, maybe a mile or better, you would eventually come to one of the many crisscross gravel roads used by farmers to access their fields. However, the criminals forced her to go cross-furrow, which meant she was probably wandering in circles. Darkness had come quickly and with it, cold breezes. An hour later, scattered moving lights appeared in the field. Searchers called her name. Shivering, she figured the authorities had finally found her wallet and the abandoned car in the school lot. Yet every time she managed to arrive at where the lights had been they were gone.

Shannon heard stalks rustling. The two convicts pushed aside corn plants.

"It's time now, you bitch!" A fist punched her in the chin. She lost her footing and flew backwards.

Attracted by the voice, something large crashed through the field from the rear. She gasped as a tall four-legged creature, as black as India ink, and monstrously huge, straddled her supine body.

A shocked curse came from one of the men. "Jesus!"

Her eyes swept up along hoofs, fetlocks, cannons, and hocks. A horse. It smelled of primordial sulfur and iron. Head directly under its groin, Shannon's mind recognized... a stallion.

One of the men raised her daddy's old shotgun. The animal reared, struck out. The sound of steel striking steel echoed down the rows. The gun soared off spinning like a propeller. A burst of gelatinous fire five feet long blew out of the animal's nostrils and lit up the dark.

A convict screamed. The man's hands slapped at the flames devouring his face. Hooves slashed air; a sound like metal hitting bone and the attacker went down. The second convict cursed and ran. The stallion pursued. Dry stalks snapped and crackled. Another fluttering flare of fire cut off a shriek. The blaze set jagged shadows dancing. A pounding, stomping, earthquake vibration that seemed to have no end followed.

Car lights appeared. Shannon rose and ran. The end of the field neared. From behind her came the sound of the demon stallion. The headlights grew brighter. Thighs burning, chest heaving, her body hit the wall. She stopped and turned. Down the cornrow came the coal-black horse. Its eyes pulsing with flame, as unstoppable as a locomotive. She turned to run again.

Hardly slowing, the pooka thrust its head between her legs, scooped up the woman, and let her slide down its neck. Shannon knotted her fingers into its mane, as soft and strong as the finest silk. Stretching legs propelled them at a speed that glued Shannon's to its back. Feelings of terror began to be replaced by exhilaration. The creature's body felt hot, its flesh warming her like an electric blanket set on high.

The wraith broke out of the field, shedding remnants of corn stalks and dross. Shannon could see the silhouette of a sheriff's deputy in the blaze of light coming from a patrol car's headlights and flashers. The man flopped on his face as the stallion threatened to run through him.

The demon increased speed. The cruiser's lights blinded Shannon. Just as she thought they would crash, the horse soared. She whooped and laughed. Everything lapsed into slow motion. The stars overhead stretched out into long strings of light. The devil animal floated over the eighteen-foot-long Crown Vic. They touched down. Turning in its own length, the stallion shook itself sideways. Shannon tumbled off and hit the ground. The huge head dropped to her level. The flame in its eyes flared. It spun and disappeared into the darkness.

🖝

Father Donahey knocked out the dottle and repacked his pipe. He retrieved a bottle of Templeton Rye, another product of his adopted state's fertility, from a side table. Pouring two fingers worth into a small glass, he warmed the eighty-proof liquor between his palms before sipping. The second confession had confirmed the first. The reported facts and another reliable witness made it hard for him to deny or misinterpret the story.

A frightened sheriff's deputy, Shawn Morgan, had followed the creature's four-foot wide swath of destruction through the cornfield to find the remains of the two escapees.

"Father," he whispered, from the other side of the confessional screen, "I'd not seen the like. The dead men were pounded into the earth. We weren't even sure they were human at first. Besides being minced into pudding, what was left still smoldered. They had been burned over half their bodies. Their flesh appeared to have been gnawed on.

"And the horse. Black as the blackest night, eyes afire, it raced over me and leaped lengthwise over my patrol car with room to spare. Must have been twenty hands high, if not more. No plow horse could move like that. The hoof prints were cut deep into the ground with knife edges."

"Where was your boss, the recently-elected Madison County sheriff, all this time?"

"I spotted him at daylight coming out of the field as naked as a jaybird. Inside the cornfield, we found his clothes, boots, and hat all in rags and tatters, as if they had exploded from the inside out. Hoof prints led away from the site. He swore me to secrecy. I don't know what to believe. Father, do you think the Sheriff could be possessed?"

Setting down the empty whisky glass, Father Donahey read from the book spread on his lap.

> The Pooka: A Celtic fairy known as a magical shape-shifter. Able to take many forms, human and animal, it is usually seen as a coal-black horse with wild mane and burning amber eyes. A high-spirited demon, it frequently takes solitary humans for wild rides. In its equine manifestation, it enjoys running through crop fields and knocking down fences.
>
> Pooka is from the old Irish 'Puca', which means goblin. The most feared fairy in Ireland, it appears only at night. The Pooka can bring both good and bad fortune. While the spirit is generally thought to be more fun loving than evil, there are stories of Pookas killing and eating their victims.

The old priest wondered what he should do. As he remembered, Sheriff Rick, although an avowed Catholic, had never been inside the church — never entered consecrated ground.

And, in spite of being a rabid Harley man, had never been present at the annual blessing of the motorcycles. The sheriff also operated the only commercial stable in the county — one more horse-shaped creature roaming around his place would attract no attention.

Perhaps Donahey should send a report up through the church hierarchy. Would they send an exorcist? Perhaps they would not believe a doddering old man. Whatever happened, his peace and that of the community would be disrupted. He stared across the room. The face of a forgiving Christ glowed from a painting hanging on the walnut-paneled wall. He counted to ten. No revelation came.

In this case, justice had been served — the kidnapped and almost raped Shannon rescued unharmed. The two convicts had met an appropriate end. Civil law represented by the unharmed deputy had been respected. Evil had been eliminated. Interesting, he thought, the sheriff's oath of office to protect and serve the community evidently bound the alternate demon personality as much as its human counterpart.

Father Ignatius Donahey smoothed out the page and closed the book. He would wait. Deep in his heart, there still resided the wide-eyed boy listening to the tales of his grandfather before the peat-fed fire of the Old Country.

The Case of the Sour Wine

The digital temperature gauge in the dash of the pickup read fifty-six degrees, up from the overnight low of forty. It was October in Iowa and the temperature rolled up and down the scale seemingly at random. Fluctuations of thirty degrees or better could occur even within a single day. Father Donahey wasn't used to such radical changes. His native Ireland could get chilly, but the climate stayed reasonable due to the warm ocean currents kissing its island shores. That and his many years in the hot humidity of South American parishes left him with no comprehension of the prairie winter to come. He wondered whether he had made the right decision in retiring to the town of Winterset, Iowa.

On top of it all, his brain measured in Celsius, not the foreign Sassenach Fahrenheit. Numbers rattled and spun in Father Donahey's head. He had tried to memorize the conversion formula but doing math in his head had never been his forte. Finally, Father Brown, the younger priest, had pulled a conversion chart off the Internet for his use. His fellow father also warned him of the dangers of the coming season with below zero temperatures, raging blizzards, and deadly winds. Any one by itself was bad enough, but the hybrid ferocity of any two or all three in combination could be killing. As the more experienced colleague, Father Brown had taken him to the local Walmart to outfit him with long underwear, flannel-lined jeans, sweaters, a polyester-quilted parka, and Gore-Tex lined gloves and boots.

The 4 x 4 Ram truck hit a bump in the gravel road and brought the elderly priest out of his reverie. "Well, Father, as I said, I hope you can help us. On the twenty-fifth, we'll be hosting Octoberfest at the winery. Our finances will be in deep doodoo if we fail. It has taken twenty years of backbreaking work to cultivate the finest grapes and ferment the most prize-winning wines in the state. Now we're about to lose it all."

"Bruno Kurz, I can hardly credit your story. It seems incredible."

"I know, Father, and if we weren't desperate, we wouldn't lay this at your feet. My wife, one of your parishioners, insisted you'd be the man to consult."

Father Donahey knew Ailene as a member of St. Joseph's congregation. She'd married out of the faith and out of her Irish bloodline. Ailene's husband Bruno was of German descent and a Lutheran. Well, times change, he thought. The day when a non-Catholic spouse was required to convert or at least promise to raise any children in the faith was gone. Given the old country history of religious bigotry, wars, and conflicts, perhaps it was for the best.

"Well, tell me the story again and leave nothing out."

"It was like I said. Our wine has made great headway in the last decade, winning prizes and competing with California and European vintages. We are one of almost a hundred licensed wineries in Iowa. At one time, before Prohibition, the state was the sixth largest wine producer in the country. The industry is finally coming back with help from Iowa State University, which has developed the cold-hardy grapes needed."

A gust of driven air whistled as it enveloped the vehicle's side mirrors. Shreds and pieces of cornshucks juggled by the wind rasped over the truck's blue pearl paint. Donahey shifted his eyes from the miles of yellow-brown corn stubble rolling past to his companion. "Bruno. You don't need to sell me on the industry. We stock your gold-medal shiraz and silver-medal merlot in the rectory pantry. Let's fast-forward to the important part."

"It was Ailene that noticed the problem two months ago. Our new computer-based inventory system kept reporting shortages — gallons of wine missing. Much more than spillage or evaporation would account for. We investigated and quickly dismissed employee pilferage. Our efforts remained at a standstill until one of our viticulturist assistants reported noticing a fast-moving shadow among the great storage barrels. We put closed-circuit cameras in the cellar. When Ailene and I viewed the recordings, we spotted a small animal fiddling with the kegs."

Father Donahey raised his hands. "And that was when you placed a trap."

"Right you are. We ordered a Havaheart model #1081 through Amazon."

A figure of a large-bosomed woman dressed in armor and pulling back a bow appeared in Father Donahey's mind. He quickly dismissed the image.

"We assembled it in the cellar, covered it with a quilt, and baited it with a bowl of our best rosé. The screeching and yowling that tumbled us out of our bed at 3:00 in the morning let us know we'd captured something."

Bruno stopped talking. Frowning, he gulped and continued. "Inside the cage, kicking and spitting, was a little man, not one and a half feet in height, dressed all in mottled green clothing."

Father Donahey shook his head and furrowed his brows. It made no more sense hearing the story's punch line a second time than it did the first.

"We were astounded, of course. Ailene was even more shocked when she recognized a few of the words the midget was spouting as Gaelic. That's when she insisted I fetch you."

The Dodge truck thumped over a cattle guard, ground its way up a sun-bleached asphalt-paved driveway, and came to a stop at the double front doors of the winery. The stoop and two dozen picnic tables in the outside area were festooned with pumpkins, gourds, and fake vines. A platform with tri-pod-mounted speakers stood waiting for the bands the couple had booked for the fall celebration. The building itself rose one story from the ground with a long slanted shake-shingled roof and mustard-colored rough-plastered walls. From the porch, Donahey could see parallel lines of pruned grape vine trunks stretching in long rows over the rolling hills of the farm.

Bruno continued his tale as they departed the truck and stepped up to the porch. He reached for a brass doorknob in the shape of a horse's head. "And on top of it all, Father, the wine and the craft beer we brewed for the festival went bad. The wine turned into vinegar and the beer developed such a vile aftertaste you cannot drink more than one gulp. We will be ruined. You have got to help us."

*

Father Donahey sat in an antique crosscut oak rocker, elbow on one of the chair's arms, chin held in his right hand. He stared at the cage and its occupant, now free of the disguising quilt. The creature inside stared back.

Legs splayed out in front of him, the captive sat in a box 42" x 15" x 15" made of twelve-gage steel mesh. His dimensions true to Bruno's description: about eighteen inches tall with head, chest, and limbs in proportion. Donahey sniffed; the creature's body scent similar to fresh-cut hay. However, the breath that whiffed across the space between them a not-so-nice combination of old stale wine and tobacco smoke.

The staring contest took place in an underground chamber that ran the length and breadth of the building. A ramp at one end led to a set of doors, which could be opened to load trucks. Around three-quarters of the room's perimeter stood brown wooden casks, double stacked, one above the other. The remaining wall space held floor to ceiling racks. Hundreds of nondescript long-necked bottles sheathed in brown corrugated paper wrappers lay on their sides, nested on the shelves. A line of four-lamp fluorescent fixtures fixed to the ceiling provided bright warm light. The room was dry and cool; Father Donahey guessed 20 to 22 Celsius degrees. Bruno and Ailene had explained the aging wine must be protected from ultraviolet light, humidity, and heat.

The couple had provided a wool tartan shawl to warm his shoulders and left him to examine the problem. The little man in the cage continued to stare back, arms crossed and the collar of his cut-away jacket turned up. A shirt bound at the neck with a string tie, vest, trousers, and scarred brogans all in various shades of emerald green completed his outfit. Everything sized to fit a human toddler.

Father Donahey decided to wait the creature out. Fifteen minutes passed. The being's tiny lips pressed together. He stroked his beard, sighed, and spoke.

"*Dia duit, Sagart.*"

It is Gaelic all right, Donahey thought. He reached deep into his memory and translated the English — good day, to you, stranger — and replied "*Dea-lá a thabhairt duit, choimhthi-och.*"

The little man squinted up his eyes and made a nasty gesture with his fingers. "*Tá mé aon choimhthiock anseo.*"

"So, you are not a stranger here. You must tell me the entire story. But first, my Gaelic is that of a child's recollection, and it's been fifty years since I used it last. Do you speak English? *An bhfuiil Béarla agat?*"

"Ter be sure, Oi speak the local tongue. Do ye think me a fool?"

"Tell me who you are."

"Well now, that's fer me ter know and ye ter find out."

Donahey noticed that the little fellow had crosshatched burn marks matching the cage grating on the back of one hand and his left cheek. "How did you get those burns? Do you need first aid?"

"Oi'm afraid iron an' me kind have a great dislike fer each other. Let me out, an' Oi'll be treatin' me own wounds."

Deciding to brave the question, Father Donahey threw out the most pressing thought, "Do we have a leprechaun here? One who cannot use his magic when surrounded by cold iron?"

"Oi was greedy ... an' shit-faced. The champion rosé — a great temptation."

"So, you have been hiding in the basement, stealing wine, and now taking your vengeance on an innocent, hard-working couple. They are about to lose their entire life's work due to a demon sponging off their achievements."

"Now, now, Father, suren it's a fact that Oi've paid me way. Me powers have made the grapes grow sweet, adjusted the blend of juice, and perfected the fermentation. Oi've even kept away the blight and the fungus that thrives in this wet land. Do ye think that pair a' blunderin' blockheads would have won all those medals without me?"

"And the missing gallons of wine?"

The little fellow wiggled bushy eyebrows. "Only fair rewards for me work."

"And the turning of wine and beer into undrinkable dregs?"

"Tis a tragedy, such as the bard William used ter write. With me imprisoned behind cold iron the drink turns into what it would be without me."

"So, if we let you out, the contents of bottle and keg would return to their original state."

"Aye, with a wave of me hand." The little man demonstrated. A tiny finger hit the side of the cage. A puff of smoke emerged, "Ouch!" He sucked on the wound.

"That reminds me, what about the three wishes? If a human captures a leprechaun, isn't the sprite bound to grant wishes? And what about the rumored pot of gold?"

"Bah, strictly human additions ter the legend. If Oi had a pot of gold, Oi'd be rentin' in Trump Tower an' eatin' off room service an' callin' the escort agencies. Me one an' only great talent is makin' things ferment."

Donahey gave voice to a thought that had been bouncing in the back of his mind. "Can we make a deal here? One to benefit all parties."

A clever smile fastened on the leprechaun's face. "Let me out an' all will be well."

The tales of his boyhood returned. Making a deal with such folk required clear thinking about the consequences. The little people would honor the letter of their deals, but you could not leave them any wiggle room in the language. Father Donahey pulled out his Meerschaum pipe and tobacco pouch.

"Let's start with your name."

The little man licked his lips and drew a miniature hand-made corncob pipe from a vest pocket. "The answer ter that question will cost ye a filled pipe."

Donahey took the little man's corncob, filled its acorn-sized bowl, and handed it back. Clicking open his ancient Zippo he sucked flame into the Meerschaum. The scent of rum-flavored smoke filled the room. The leprechaun stuck his pipe out through the mesh. Donahey held the lighter, yellow-blue flame flickered. "I am Father Patrick Ignatius Donahey and, your name?"

With a disgusted look, the captive said, "Tis Bleery,"

"The entire name, please." Father Donahey moved the lighter closer.

"Bleery Merry O' Lanigan."

"Your age and birthplace?"

Bleery puffed out smoke. "At me last birthday Oi was one thousand. In yer years, Oi'm in me twenties. Born and raised in County Cork an' came ter this country durin' the famine. An' a nasty rough ocean trip it was."

The two smoked and enjoyed some quiet time. Bleery broke the silence. "Ye know, suren it would be grand if we had a bit of spirit ter share — like what's in that flask in yer side pocket."

Father Donahey's eyebrows went up. Well, why not, thought

the priest. It might even make the leprechaun easier to deal with. He pulled out the screw top, leather-bound flask and took a swig. The Templeton Rye went down smoothly. He found a drinking straw among the festival supplies on a nearby table, which allowed Bleery to take a pull without touching the cage mesh.

"Aye, that be splendid stuff. Now, about our business proposition, Oi'm thinkin', a straight-forward approach. Ye let me out, I fix the wine an' beer, an' all is forgiven."

"And what's to prevent you from taking revenge, or running off and leaving the deserving couple with disaster? Now here is my thought: We let you out, you restore the spirits, and you convert to Catholicism. As a good Christian, you would have to obey The Golden Rule."

Leprechaun cheeks, nose, and lips formed a look of horror. He folded his arms across his chest. Beard flapping in his haste to reply, he said. "If Oi did that, Oi'd turn into one of yer big-boned, large-assed, short-lived humans. No, no, not fer me."

"Then your chances of leaving that cage are greatly diminished. Of course, we could turn you over to the scientists at Iowa State University. They'd love to have a test subject like you. I can see it now. A cluster of white-coated men and women taking blood samples, doing x-rays, poking and prodding. A healthy life it will be with no booze, no evil tobacco, and balanced meals. Of course, at some point there would be the dissection. School officials might even be pleased enough to compensate the Kurz couple for their losses."

Bleery's lips tightened. He shivered. Tiny drops of sweat appeared on his forehead. Brows furrowed, then relaxed. His arms uncrossed. "Father, Oi can tell yer a fair man. Let me propose a wee contest. If ye win, Oi'll do as ye please. If Oi win, ye let me go with no obligation."

"What did you have in mind?"

"We tell jokes, Irish jokes. A warm-up round an' then two

out of three ter win."

Father Donahey figured he had had many years of telling funny stories in his homilies, lectures, and sermons. He had a whole box of joke books stored back at the church collected over the years. Besides, if he lost, they would be no worse off. In addition, there was a soul to save here — perhaps his first convert in this new land. "Okay, I'll do it. Let's flip a coin to see who goes first."

"Bejiggers, if ye ain't a sportin' man." Bleery tossed a coin through the mesh.

Donahey checked both sides. On one face of the patinaed metal was stamped a profile of Nero, the Roman emperor of around 60 AD. He scratched the surface with a fingernail, revealing gold color. He frowned and looked with lowered eyebrows at the leprechaun.

Catching the priest's thoughts, Bleery responded. "Tis one of a kind, an *aureus*. Me grandfather found it long ago in the ruins of Vindolanda close up to Hadrian's Wall."

"You call it — heads or tails. The loser goes first." Donahey flipped the coin.

A shout of "Heads!" came from the leprechaun.

Donahey slapped the coin on the back of his wrist. He raised his hand. "Tails it is. I start the warm-up round."

The Father began his story. "Now, Michael Hoolihan was courting Frances Phelan. The young couple sat in the parlor of the girl's house night after night, much to the annoyance of old man Phelan. One night he couldn't take any more. Standing at the top of the stairs, he yelled down, 'Daughter, what's that young fella doin' here all hours of the night?' 'Why, Dad,' said Frances, 'Michael was just tellin' me everythin' that's in his heart!' 'Well, next time,' roared Phelan, 'just let him tell ye what's in his head, an' it won't take half as long!'"

The leprechaun chortled. "Now, that's a goody but an oldie. Here's a better."

"For a holiday, Mulvaney decided ter go ter Switzerland ter

fulfill a lifelong dream to climb the Matterhorn. He hired a guide an' just as they neared the top, the men were caught in a snow slide. Three hours later, a Saint Bernard plowed through ter them, a keg of brandy tied under its chin. 'Hooray!' shouted the guide. 'Here comes man's best friend!' 'Yeah,' said Mulvaney. 'An' look at the size of the dog that's bringin' it!'"

Father Donahey chuckled, "Well, I have to admit you bested me on that one. Let's go to the first round."

"You lost, so you start," replied Bleery, clapping his hands.

"Okay, how about his one. Father Murphy walks into a pub in Donegal, and says to the first man he meets, 'Do you want to go to heaven?' The man said, 'Oi do, Father.' The priest said, 'Then stand over there against the wall.' Then the priest asked the second man, 'Do you want to go to heaven?' 'Certainly, Father,' was the man's reply. 'Then stand over there against the wall,' said the priest. Then Father Murphy walked up to O'Toole and said, 'Do you want to go to heaven?' O'Toole said, 'No, Oi don't Father.' The priest said, 'I don't believe this. You mean to tell me that when you die you don't want to go to heaven.' O'Toole said, 'Oh, when Oi die, yes. Suren, Oi thought ye were gettin' a group together ter go right now.'"

The leprechaun pursed his lips and winked. "Not bad, not bad at all." He launched into his next joke.

"McQuillan walked into a bar an' ordered martini after martini, each time removin' the olives an' placin' them in a jar. When the jar was filled with olives an' all the drinks downed, the Irishman started ter leave. 'S'cuse me,' said a customer, who was puzzled over what McQuillan had done. 'What was that all about?' 'Nothin', said the Irishman, 'me wife just sent me out fer a jar o' olives.'"

"Those are close to a tie," Father Donahey said.

"Search your heart, Father. You know mine was the better."

"Okay, you have the first round." As the loser, the priest began the second round.

"Brenda O'Malley is home as usual, making dinner, when

Tim Finnegan arrives at her door. 'Brenda, may I come in?' he asks. 'I've somethin' ter tell ye.' 'Of course, ye can come in, yer always welcome, Tim. But where's me husband?' 'That's what I'm here ter be tellin' ye, Brenda. There was an accident down at the Guinness brewery....' 'Oh, God no!" cries Brenda. 'Please don't tell me....' 'Suren I must, Brenda. Your husband Seamus is dead an' gone. I'm sorry.' Brenda reached a hand out to her side, found the arm of the rocking chair by the fireplace, pulled the chair to her, and collapsed into it. She wept for many minutes. Finally, she looked up at Tim. 'How did it happen, Tim?' 'It was terrible, Brenda. He fell into a vat of Guinness Stout an' drowned.' 'Oh, my dear Jaysus! But ye must tell me true, Tim. Did he at least go quickly?' 'Well, no, Brenda... no.' 'No?' 'Fact is, he got out three times ter pee.'"

Slapping his knee, Bleery's chuckle turned into a long stuttering laugh, joined by Father Donahey's. A male voice shouted down from the upstairs. "Are you two all right?"

Donahey answered, "Bruno, we're fine. Situation on the way to resolution, need a few more minutes." The door shut. "Okay, Bleery, your turn."

"Well, Father, remember our agreement, if Oi win this round, Oi get me freedom. This is one of me best. Two Irish lads had been out shackin' up with their girl friends. One felt guilty an' decided he should stop at the church an' confess. He went into the confession booth an' told the priest, 'Father, Oi have sinned. I have committed fornication with a lady. Please forgive me.' The Father said, 'Tell me who the lady was.' The lad said he couldn't do that an' the Father said he couldn't grant him forgiveness unless he did. 'Was it Mollie O'Grady?' asked the Father. 'No.' 'Was it Rosie Kelly?' 'No.' 'Was it that red-headed wench Tessie O'Malley?' 'No.' 'Well then,' said the Father, 'You'll not be forgiven.' When the lad met his companion outside the friend asked, 'So, did ye find forgiveness?' 'No,' said the other, 'but Oi picked up three good prospects!'"

The joke produced no response from the Father, not even a

smile. "Oh, oh," said Bleery, "Oi think Oi lost that round."

"That you did. The score now is one to one. Since you lost you need to go first."

The leprechaun bit his lower lip, knuckled his forehead, and took a full minute to prepare.

"Two leprechauns went ter the convent an' begged an audience with the Mother Superior. 'Well, how can I help you little people?' asked Mother Superior. The larger and more intelligent of the leprechauns asked, 'Oh Mother Superior, would ye be knowin' of any midget nuns here at the convent?' 'No,' says Mother Superior, 'I don't have any midget nuns here at the convent.' 'All right then, Mother Superior, would ye be knowin' of any midget nuns in all of Ireland then?' 'No, no,' replied Mother Superior, 'I don't know of any nuns who are also midgets in all of Ireland at all.' 'Well then, Mother Superior, in all of nundom, in the whole world of all nuns, would ye be knowin', then, of any midget nuns?' 'No, I would not, there are no midget nuns in the whole of the world!' replied Mother Superior, 'an' would you please tell me what this is all about?' The askin' leprechaun turned sadly ter the stupid leprechaun an' said 'See, tis as Oi told ye all along, ye've been datin' a penguin.'"

Donahey smiled and spoke, "It's not an old Irish joke, since they didn't commonly know about penguins long ago. But it's reasonably funny. Let's see what I can do."

"Padraic Flaherty came home drunk every evening toward ten. Now, the Missus was never too happy about it, either. So, one night she hides in the cemetery and figures to scare the bee-jeezus out of him. As poor Pat wanders by, up from behind a tombstone she jumps out in a red devil costume screaming, 'Padraic Sean Flaherty, suren ye don't give up yer drinkin' an' it's ter Hell I'll take ye.' Pat, undaunted, staggered back and demanded, 'Who the hell are ye?' To that the Missus replied, 'I'm the divil, ye damned old fool.' To which Flaherty remarked, 'Damned glad ter meet ye, sir, I'm married ter yer sister.'"

Bleery's hands trembled. He let out a half hiss, half titter. "Oi like it, but Oi can't make up me mind. It seems like a tie ter me. We need ter go another round."

"I think I had the edge on you this round, but not by much. To be absolutely fair, I'll agree to a substitute round. The score remains one-to-one. You first."

With a wan smile and a bit of despair in his voice Bleery launched into his next joke.

"Pat and Mike were city employees an' one warm day they were workin' on street repair. Just across the street was a house of prostitution. As they worked, they saw the Baptist minister walk down the street an' enter the house. Pat says, 'Mike, suren did ye see what that dirty hypocrite of a Baptist minister just did? He went into that house of ill repute.'" Mike shook his head and said, 'Yer can never tell what ye might see around here.' A few minutes later, a Methodist preacher walked up an' entered the house. Pat slaps his head with his hand, and says, 'Mike, did ye see that? Did ye see what that heathen Methodist just did? Suren, he went into that house.' Mike just shook his head an' said, 'What's this world comin' ter?' A bit later Father O'Brien, from their parish, entered the house, an' Pat said, 'Mike, tis like Oi been tellin' ye, there's somebody sick in that house.'"

Father Donahey had been waiting for this moment, his final joke already selected from the beginning. He hoped it would do. This last one of Bleery's would be difficult to beat.

Sweat soaked through his shirt and into the armpits of his jacket. He removed the shawl and laid it aside. He clasped his hands together for a brief silent prayer, whispered "Amen," and crossed himself. He began his last joke of the last round with a voice increasing in confidence.

"As soon as she had finished convent school, a bright young girl named Lena shook the dust of Ireland off her shoes and made her way to New York where, before long, she became a successful performer in show business. Eventually she returned to her hometown for a visit, and on Saturday night went to confession in the church, which she had always attended as a child. In the confessional, Father Sullivan recognized her and asked about her work. She explained that she was an acrobatic dancer, and he wanted to know what that meant. Lena said she would be happy to show him the kind of thing she did on stage. She stepped out of the confessional and within sight of Father Sullivan, she went into a series of cartwheels, leaping splits, handsprings, and back flips. Kneeling near the confessional, waiting their turn, were two middle-aged ladies. They witnessed Lena's acrobatics with wide eyes, and one said to the other: 'Will ye just look at the penance Father Sullivan is givin' out this night, an' me without me bloomers on!'"

There was a choking noise; the leprechaun's body was shaking. Both hands covered his mouth. Father Donahey laughed aloud. The contagious mirth beat down the last of Bleery's resistance. A great bray of a guffaw announced his surrender.

Donahey retrieved a bottle of Evian water from the supply table and blessed it. He opened the cage door. Bleery danced out and dodged between his legs. The Father grabbed his collar. The imp pulled his arms out and left the jacket in the priest's hands.

"Hold now, you need to live up to your promise."

The little man ran past the stacked wine barrels, the priest in close pursuit, and shouted over his shoulder. "Oi will, Father, but we didn't say when Oi would convert. Like O'Toole in the story, Oi'm not ready to go yet."

Donahey made a grab. The buttons on the leprechaun's shirt popped off. He rolled his shoulders, leaving the shirt in the hands of his pursuer.

"Bejiggers, man, will ye strip me buck naked?"

The two danced back and forth, Donahey keeping his smaller quarry from gaining the exits at either end of the aisle. The little man turned and dove between the stacked wine casks, his small size allowing him sanctuary. Donahey stretched an arm into the space. Bleery slapped it away. He slipped off his suit coat and tried again. This time the imp bit his index finger. Donahey jerked back his arm.

"Well, suren if we don't have a standoff, Father."

Donahey pressed his lips together and retrieved the bottle of holy water from his coat. "Tis not as much of a standoff as you might believe, me bucko."

The priest unscrewed the cap. He began to recite a blessing and squeezed the plastic bottle, spraying its contents over the trapped sprite.

*

Father Donahey sat in his favorite leather wingback chair, a journal open on his lap. He had taken to writing down his experiences with the supernatural. So far, there were two separate cases, the first featuring a pooka, the second a leprechaun. The adventures had avoided disaster and seemed to work out in the end.

He mused about the ending of the latest story. The little man had lost the joke contest and emerged from his cage to be converted and blessed. No longer submerged in magic, in a few months he put on weight and grew into a healthy human male five foot four inches tall. The ex-sprite had kept his talent for fermenting wine. Donahey thought of it as the 'green thumb' some humans seemed to possess. Plants of all kinds grew large and productive in the presence of those blessed with the talent. Lacking the ability, Father Donahey had always thought of it as a form of magic.

Recognizing his contribution, the Kurnzs had given Bleery a share in the business. Their Octoberfest was a great success. The three of them formed a fine partnership and the winery continued to prosper. Bleery (now known by his baptized name Blair) had also retained his gift of gab, and when the glamour was upon him could attract the women.

The priest in Father Donahey looked forward to hearing some interesting confessions from the former leprechaun in the future. He closed the journal and knocked out the dottle remaining in his pipe into a woven bamboo wastebasket. He finished the last drops of the winery's prize merlot in the glass on his side table, rose, and walked over to his old roll top desk. The journal went into a drawer locked with a key. He rattled down the top and locked it as well. Donahey stretched his arms wide, yawned, and left the rectory study. On his way upstairs to bed, he wondered again how this fertile land could grow such wondrous crops, people, and enchantments.

Batman and Catwoman

Dry, heavily-laden cornstalks rustled and crackled in the fields. Husk-wrapped ears hid the gold beneath from the weak fall sun. Skeletal leaves caressed each other, offering good-byes as they sensed the vibration of a combine coming their way. A crisp breeze bounced along the gravel farm-to-market road disbursing the knee-high gray dust created by the tire-crush of tractors and grain trucks.

Dressed in his civvies, old knee-worn jeans and a gray hoody, Father Ignatius Patrick Donahey tooled along the road's bald spots riding the parish's 1960 model Schwinn Panther II bicycle. Its out-of-the-box 'radiant red' paint now as drab as the third-generation black no-nonsense tires that had replaced the original whitewalls. Rust spotted the chrome fenders, and a hole existed in the tank where the horn button once poked out. The twin headlights were now merely decorative, the in-side works eaten by an acid leak from old batteries. Front and back carriers, bent from use, remained functional. One held the father's small basket of lunch and a scarred coffee ther-mos. The fifty-five-year-old machine and he made a good fit. The exterior marks of their old age hid the still strong hearts inside.

He grunted and stood up on the pedals, utilizing his body weight to help power the bike up the hill before him. Outland-ers, if they thought of Iowa at all, believed it to be flat as a tabletop. They were quickly discouraged of that fallacy if they became one of the thousands of bicycle riders in the Register's Annual Great Bike Ride Across Iowa. These rolling plains were good, he thought, to get the heart pumping and then back to calm on the downhill ride, until the next looming hillock.

It was a different land from the Irish backcountry of his birth. From the top of the hill, he could see to the horizon. A veritable sea of corn, sitting only five hundred feet above what had been a giant inland sea ages ago — if the geologists were to be believed. The murmur of corn harmonizing with the purr of the far-off combine caught his ears, a mantra relaxing him, reminding him of the service he had once attended in a Tibetan Buddhist temple in India. He let out a long breath. Those years and many more gone now, his natal village nothing but fallen stones and rotting thatch, he had chosen to retire, replant, and rediscover himself at St. Joseph's Church in the small town of Winterset, Iowa. His only remaining priestly responsibility: to fill in when the local priest was sick or traveling.

A flicker of motion caught his eye. Someone or something animate trotted over the top of the second hill down the line. Father Donahey pushed off. Vigorous pedaling added extra speed to help with the climb up the next slope. The old bike and older passenger hit the summit of the next hill with energy to spare. The Schwinn vibrated like an excited beagle fully involved in the chase. The partners, mechanical and biological, picked up speed. The Father let out a whoop of encouragement. Fenders rattling, the pair descended from the second hill. The blinding tears the wind of passage brought to Donahey's eyes caused him to miss the natural gravel ramp chewed out by vehicle tires at the bottom. The bike hit the obstacle at what Father Donahey later estimated to be twenty KPH.

Man and machine went airborne. Donahey's howl of fear came from between gritted teeth. Loss of gravity at the apogee caused the Father's breakfast of orange juice and peanut butter toast to rise in his stomach. Hands death-gripped the handlebars. Feet reversed the pedals, too late to apply brakes that only worked with earth contact. In passing, the high rider looked down on the head of the person he had spotted two hills ago. Time seemed suspended.

During his adrenaline-extended descent through the air, he recognized the walker as William Gottschald. The six-foot-tall, heavily muscled farm boy was one of his parishioners. The bike smacked into the roadbed, Donahey's teeth clacked together, he felt as though his skeleton was trying to exit his body through the anus. He watched his lunch basket detach and fly to the right. The bike's balloon tires compressed against the earth, cyborg man-machine flipped completely over front-to-back. The soft piled gravel on the roadside absorbed its second earth-contact. The bike skidded into the ditch and stopped.

Father Donahey dismounted, allowed the bike to fall, and staggered back onto the road. He stood with his head spinning, hair disheveled, and hands on temples.

"Wow! Father, I didn't know you could hotdog on a bike. And that one not even a BMX. You did a flip, a nose wheelie, and a slide, what a combo."

"William," Donahey groaned, "I think only the intercession of the Virgin Mary herself preserved me."

"You need to be more careful in the future, Father. That bike's tank bar could have damaged your testi... uhmm... manhood. And next time, you should wear a helmet."

Donahey staggered a few steps, picked up the lunch basket, and moved off the road up to the fence line. He leaned against a post and allowed his body to slide down, his butt compressing the feral foxtail and fescue grasses. William hunkered down at his side. They sat quietly for a moment. The young man's brows and lips formed a frown. He rubbed his hands together in a twitchy fashion. A crow sentry atop a power line cawed three times, sending the all-clear signal to the other members of his murder. The juggernaut it had spotted coming over the hill seemed at rest. Father Donahey massaged his jaw and neck.

"I do not believe I have seen you at Mass lately, my son."

William grimaced. "I'm not sure I'm worthy anymore."

Donahey's professional instinct caught the scratchy scent of guilt. In his experience, teens such as William, carried loads of nasty feelings that adults would shrug off. He sighed. Ready or not, here was someone that needed his ministration. He checked his watch, raised the basket to his lap, and shuffled the contents.

"Looks like the edibles survived. Would you be of a mind to share a sandwich with me, William? It is close to lunch time."

"Well, I don't know."

"Come now, my son, don't be shy. We'll try the coffee too, as long as you don't mind sharing the same cup."

Without waiting for a response, Donahey unwrapped a sandwich and handed half to William. "Liverwurst and mayo on whole wheat okay with you?"

The boy nodded his head yes and bit into his half. Donahey held the ancient thermos to his ear and shook it. He smiled at William, "Looks like it also survived without breakage." He unscrewed the cup; the scent of Columbian coffee mixed with something else filled their personal space.

"Father, is that Templeton Rye I smell spicing the coffee?"

"And how do you know what Templeton Rye smells like?"

William's silence bespoke his guilt. His knowledge probably experienced as the result of teen explorations of forbidden substances behind barns or in the back of pickup trucks. The Father was not so concerned with Iowa's Puritan laws on the drinking age, a youth this old in the Ireland of his time would have been welcomed in the local pubs and taverns. In fact, as soon as you were tall enough to slap your money on the bar, you would be served.

"Well, William, you will have to do without. Now tell me what's bothering you so much you can't come to Mass."

"I don't know Father, there's big sins involved."

"Ah, you let me be the judge of that." Donahey pulled another old chestnut out of a priest's grab bag of useful phrases. "Confession is good for the soul."

"Father, will this be like the confessional? Anything I say is only between you and God and me?"

"Of course, my son. But I can take your confession at the church tomorrow, if you wish."

The two looked up at the great blue bowl overhead, listened to the wind-music through the grasses, and inhaled the herb-scent of dried plants. The never-ending air motion of the rolling prairie tickled his arm hairs. "This is as holy a place as any," Donahey said.

William took a deep breath, clasped his hands, and placed them on his lap. "It all began with our decision to attend the Comicon held in Des Moines last week. Glad and I —"

"That would be Gladys McCann?" Donahey remembered a thin-as-a-rail, redheaded girl in the same class as William and a cross-country runner on the high school team.

"Yes, Father, we've been dating." William sat silent, gathering his thoughts.

Donahey remembered the pair as being close to the bottom rung of their peers' social structure. They had been the objects of various cruel teen jokes and bullying — some of it physical and some via Internet social media. Strangely, the bewildered couple had never fought back. Given William's muscular development, a few punches back behind the school building would probably have ended the matter. Nasty events grew in number. The principal and the school board had finally put an end to the public side of it, but that only seemed to make their tormentors more determined.

"We went costumed, Father."

"Costumed?"

"Yes, thousands of fans turn out for the event, many tricked out as their favorite TV, movie, or comic book character. We met at the event. Anyway, the evening went strange from the beginning. Glad was waiting for me just inside the Iowa Event Hall's main entrance."

*

"Glad, you look great! Catwoman, right?"

"You told me you were going as Batman. Thought I'd appear as his greatest love-villainess."

"Wow! You... you look a little — a lot filled out."

"Padding here and an uplift there does wonders."

"And the shiny black outfit?"

"Borrowed my sister's motorcycle leathers and her six-inch stiletto heels." She stroked a snake-like belt that surrounded her waist and crossed over one shoulder. "Spray painted black my brother's old Indiana Jones' whip."

Bill blushed. "Uh, one thing. I don't know how to say this."

"Yes?"

"One of your ... uh ... thingies is lower than the other."

Gladys leaned closer and giggled. "You mean one of my boobs?"

Tongue-tied, Bill nodded.

"Okay, I'll go in the women's restroom over there and make adjustments. You wait outside."

Bill leaned against the wall, keeping out of the flow of hundreds of costumed and non-costumed fans. Lots of color with blacks, reds, and blues predominating made for a slightly dizzying experience. The odors of vender food, hot dogs, nachos, French fries, and popcorn mixed with the perfume, deodorant, and sweat of the crowd. As more ticket holders pushed in, the smell changed and grew in intensity as it absorbed individual scents.

He separated out the characters he knew. Star Trek Vulcans and Klingons, a Green Arrow, several Black Widows, multitudinous zombies, the Flash, and a Captain America mingled and talked in mysterious made-up languages. A couple costumed as a tree and a raccoon wandered by. Men and women dressed as security guards with DI hats infiltrated the masses.

He wondered whether they were real or fans.

That might be neat – come dressed as a guard. You could get close to the featured guests without a ticket and into their private meetings. He might even get a free picture with the actors that portrayed Captain James Kirk, the Hulk, or Superman. Maybe he would try that next time.

Catwoman came hustling out of the restroom exit and walked by him. He rushed to catch up. He grabbed her arm. "Boy, that was fast. Usually you take a lot longer."

His date turned. The blue eyes behind the mask had an icy tint he hadn't noticed before. The arm he was holding felt more solid than it should be. She looked him up and down, noticed the muscles, and parted her lips. His shoulders retracted, eyebrows rose. The smile made him feel nervous, not welcome. An image of him as a goat facing a tiger flashed through his mind.

Bill's face flushed. He wanted to be in motion before he embarrassed himself with a foolish move or question. "Are you ready? We are on a date after all."

The woman tilted her head in a cute feline manner, exposed white pointy teeth. Muscles twitched in her jaw. Her fingers slid between his. "That would be pu-r-r-r-fect."

The hand-holding couple twisted through the packed hall, sometimes side-by-side, sometimes single file. They paused for photos when people asked. Catwoman had them take action poses with fists threatening each other, or with her whip laid across his shoulders. The most popular was a romantic pose, with her relaxing dreamily in his arms.

As they progressed, the crowd noise and need to maneuver kept conversation to a minimum. They paused here and there to view exhibits and Hollywood props for sale, some even real. His date was attracted to a table at author's row featuring Mallory Petersen mysteries, the work of writer Stephen Brayton. The series starred a kick-ass martial arts female detective.

Glad/Catwoman's eyes grew big. She stroked a book.

"Glad, I'd buy that for you, but it cost me all my cash to get our tickets."

She moved close, rubbing her body against his side. Her mouth close to his ear, she whispered. "What a delight-f-f-ful ear you have."

Her teeth gave it a nibble. Bill's arms and legs tingled. He felt the beginnings of arousal. His partner giggled. Hand on one hip, she turned to the author and selected a book.

"I'll take this one, big boy."

The author asked, "Who, emm, who should I make it out to?"

"Catwoman," she responded, leaning over to expose her cleavage and handing him a twenty.

The author grinned, more of a leer than a smile. Bill noted that his signature seemed shaky. He wondered where Glad had gotten the twenty. Her outfit had no pockets. It was very tight with no bulges to indicate hiding places.

Glad looked at him and at the book. The whisper came again. There was something both familiar and alien about the voice. It sounded like Glad yet didn't. "I've got what I came f-f-f-for, let's ditch this crowd."

They exited the Center. She led him towards the Des Moines River. They strolled along the darkened River Walk. Bill was surprised that the time had passed so quickly since their late afternoon arrival. It must be close to nine. Lights from the buildings danced along the river's surface. The air was fresh, the night cool, yet he felt more than warm enough holding Glad's hand. A damp scent redolent of fresh-cut green grass rose from the riverbanks. He inhaled. A spicy perfume came from his date. Breathing more deeply, he felt himself grow stronger, more forceful. His world shrank to a five-foot circle surrounding Glad and him.

She sensed his increasing interest. Breaking away, she ran in great bounds down the walk. He raced after, as fast as he could run. Catwoman easily maintained her lead. Not escaping, just staying within temptation range, taunting him with peels of mezzo-soprano laughter. How can she sprint like that, he thought, in those spikes?

He caught her, suddenly close. She had come to a halt, crouching; back raised, arms out with fingers formed into claws. She sniffed, and hissed — the same escaping steam-hiss he had heard from Aunt Nola's cat when confronted by a dog. Ahead, four shadows stood blocking their path. Bill shook his head, trying to expand his perception. The four stepped out into a lighted area.

"I don't think you two will be going much further. You and Gladys have given us a merry chase."

Bill blinked. Damn... if it wasn't their main tormentors, John, Carl, Kicker, and Doug, classmates come all the way from Winterset.

"You two are going to get what's coming to you. You shouldn't have got us in trouble with the school and police. Kicker, Doug, show them the quality of your black belts."

Clenching his fists, Bill said, "That's typical of you, John. The cowardly bully leader enjoys watching while his buddies do the dirty work."

"Not to worry, I'll join in before the night's over." He chortled, "Batman, just think of me as the Joker."

Kicker and Doug walked forward loose-limbed. At the eight-foot mark, they leaped. Bill took a step back and raised his fists. "Run, Glad! I'll hold 'em."

Something black and powerful cartwheeled between him and the attackers. Catwoman landed on her feet and shot a hand holding a book forward. The book spine took Kicker right under the nose. He spun away with a scream. A female hand grabbed a fist-full of Doug's shirt, pulling him forward and over her back. Female legs and thighs bent and bucked. Her opponent sailed over the guardrail and down onto the river-bank. In the shocked seconds of quiet following the toss, the five remaining on the walk heard a splash.

Carl jumped forward. A high school wrestling champion, Carl enjoyed close work. He attempted to grapple with Glad.

She grabbed a forearm and using his forward motion pulled him to one side. In passing, she punched him in the kidney — an illegal move in wrestling. Surprised and paralyzed with pain, her opponent dropped to the asphalt.

Hidden by Carl's tumbling body, a recovered Kicker lived up to his name and planted a surprise *mawashi geri*, or round-house kick, on Glad's thigh. She bounded sidewise and chuckled. "That was a good one. You won't get in a second."

A frozen Bill tried to understand how his Glad had developed such fighting skills. She and Kicker moved in a killers' duet, circling and leaping in and out. Fists blurred in punch, block, and counterpunch. Kicker pulled his favorite move, a *mae tobi geri*, jumping front kick. With a speed that made her arms invisible, Glad grabbed his ankle and flipped him onto the metal tubing of the riverside railing. An audible crack testified to a pair of broken ribs. Kicker had had enough. He held up a hand, forefinger and thumb held apart in surrender.

Catwoman's eyes narrowed. "Ha! The old mercy sign of the Roman gladiator. Haven't seen that for a few millennia." She pointed at Carl and Kicker. "Okay, but over the side go you two."

Carl crawled to Kicker's side. The pair worked their way over the rail and rolled down into the water. Bill looked down the walkway. John was gone. He felt Glad's hand grip his shoulder. He lowered his head.

"I'm ashamed. I just stood here while you did the fighting. I couldn't even help."

Fingers grasped his chin and raised his head. He looked into icy eyes. The whisper came.

"It isn't over. You will get your turn. It will be a p-p-p-leasure. Walk down the p-p-p-path," she pointed, "that way. John will come to you."

Catwoman enfolded him in her arms. One hand briefly massaged the back of his neck before pulling him down into a tongue-kiss so blatantly sexual that he achieved a pop-goes-the-weasel erection. His heart rate blew upward, nostrils expanded to take in extra oxygen, muscles responded moving his limbs and body fully into her fierce clinch. He felt full of confidence, all doubt gone. He was The Batman!

Glad broke the embrace and leaped into the bushes and the darkness. Bill trotted down the walk. On the other side of the river he recognized the Simon Estes Amphitheater and later the West Riverfront Park. He was beginning to feel a bit silly, when he heard shouting and crying. The slap of panicked footsteps came towards him.

John appeared out of the darkness. His face screwed up in a mask of fear-wide eyes and mouth. One cheek had three claw marks leaking blood. He tried to push Bill aside, only wanting to continue to escape. Spinning him around, Bill walloped him in the stomach. John, the cornered rat, punched back, hitting his opponent in the left pectoral. Bill held his enemy close and worked on the stomach, blow after blow.

The bully pushed his foe back and tried a two-handed choke-hold. Bill pushed his hands up into the open 'V' of John's arms. His thumbs went into his adversary's eyes. John released the hold and staggered back. Bill felt his muscles contract. Two hundred pounds of body backed the fist that punched John mid-face. Down he went. He lay on the cool, hard asphalt, moaning, feet twitching.

"Don't, no more — please."

The bushes parted silently. Catwoman drifted to his side. They looked at each other, smiled, and nodded. Bill lifted John into a firefighter's carry, trotted over to the river, then with a lift of hips, and a jerk of shoulders tossed a screaming John into the water below.

*

The evening's surprises weren't over. A slinky purr came to his ear, "Batman-n-n, my he-ro." A flick of the wrist and Catwoman held a mag-strip hotel key card between two fingers. He wondered where that came from. What else was hidden on her person?

Glad/Catwoman had reserved a room at the Residence Inn, just off the River Walk. In the darkened hotel suite, they took turns stripping off each other's costumes. That this partner was better fleshed than Glad escaped his notice in the heat generated by their foreplay. He had never felt so aroused. Flesh to flesh, chemical messages passed. Lips, teeth, fingers seemed to cover every square inch of their bodies. Actions Glad initiated accelerated their passion. He had only a second to wonder where she had learned all this, before a tight, clasping, warm entry. He remembered moaning (his) and yowling (hers). Minutes later the electric climax occurred, marvelous beyond all expectation. The afterglow found him completely exhausted and almost asleep.

In this dream-like state, he thought he witnessed something incredible. His partner transformed. In the light escaping from the bathroom, he witnessed Glad's breasts melt away, soft slightly protruding stomach became six-packs, hips slimmed, and internal sex organs were replaced with external genitalia. The Adam's apple became more pronounced and the body overall less curved, more angular. The resulting male creature started putting on the Batman costume. Bill's heavy eyes closed.

*

Light streamed in from partially closed blinds as, Bill woke. Something warm and cuddly lay spoon-style against his backside. He tuned to find the real Glad, naked and wide awake, sharing the hotel bed.

"Well, I didn't think you would ever wake, but the energy you burned up at our first love-making must have taken a lot out of you. It was wonderful. I didn't think you so knowledgeable."

Bill grunted and tried to shake out last night's memories.

Glad ran a hand through his tussled hair. "I thought I had lost you. When I came out of the restroom, you had disap-

peared. I looked all night, until you found me just before closing time. I suppose you were busy getting this room. You could
have told me."

"Ah, we weren't together the whole time?"

"Silly Batman, no. I just told you."

The sun stood directly overhead, its heat drawing beads of
sweat on the foreheads of Bill and Father Donahey. The breeze
reversed itself and brought corn stalk dust swirling in from the
harvesting activities in the adjacent field.

"So, Father, there must have been two Catwomen. Who was
the one on the River Walk? Glad and I both had sex, but with
whom? She believes I was her lover. The creature that borrowed my Batman costume must have gone back for her. It
used us, then placed us in bed together."

Bill hid his face in his hands. His voice came out muffled.

"They wanted us to think we spent the night in each other's
arms. The fights occurred. I saw the terrible foursome yesterday. They were all bandaged up and wouldn't make eye contact."

The machine-whack and engine-prattle of the combine drew
close, making it hard for Father Donahey to hear. Dust settled
on his clothes and made him cough.

"My son, we need to continue this later. I will think about
what you have said. In the meantime, my call is that you have
sinned. Maybe not so much for the fighting — that seems to
have worked out a problem for the entire community. The pre-
marital sex, however — common now-a-days, but sinful still."

Donahey placed a friendly hand on Bill's shoulder. "However, my son, there is plenty of room for forgiveness. Let us hope
that there will be no unplanned pregnancy. I will give you your
penance later. Convince Gladys to come and see me, and me
only, for her confession."

Father Donahey removed the pipe from his mouth and

practiced blowing a smoke ring. He sat in his old wingback leather chair with an ancient book open on his lap. If his conclusion was correct, Bill and Gladys had been luckier than they could possibly imagine. The clue that gave him the answer to the riddle was the boy's recollection of the metamorphoses of the Catwoman creature into a male. His eyes fell to the book.

> Succubus/incubus: A demon, a supernatural creature, an enchantress or seducer of men and women — the succubus, being the female version and the incubus the male counterpart. The demons are suspected of feeding on the soul-energy of humans through sexual intercourse. In several early accounts, the demon is described as one entity, capable of shapeshifting back and forth between male and female bodies and personalities. Repeated sexual activity with a succubus or incubus may result in the loss of health, abnormal mental disorders, addictive sexual behavior, or even death.
>
> These creatures are generally supposed to be sterile and unable to reproduce. However, some sources indicate that the female wraith will collect the sperm of males to be used later by the male version to impregnate his female victims. A succubus usually takes the form of a beautiful woman or man, but upon closer inspection may display deformities such as claws, fangs, or snake-like tails.
>
> While most accounts picture succubae as malevolent, a few tales exist where the demon rescues or assists humans in trouble.

*

Donahey shook his head. He wondered what kind of country he had chosen to live in. So far, he had run into a sheriff-cum-pooka, a leprechaun in the Kurz's vineyard, and now a succubus. All were creatures that possessed evil reputations but had intentionally chosen to do good when they could have done the opposite. Perhaps these fallen dark angels occasionally remembered the days when they were protectors of humankind.

He took a sip of Templeton Rye and stared into the face of the smiling cherub carved into the bowl of his Meerschaum pipe. There was nothing in his power, or anyone else's, that could change what had taken place. Therefore, they must ameliorate the consequences. Gladys's story had been shorter but supportive of Bill's account. Her seduction had come out just as romantic and as sexually gratifying. The difference, she still thought her partner throughout was Bill.

His concern for her — a possible pregnancy. However, if the book was correct Bill would be the father, even though the conception took place through a third party. It would be sort of like artificial insemination. If it happened, he was sure Bill would do the honorable thing. In the meantime, it would be well for the boy to keep what happened in his missing hours secret. No one, and especially Gladys, would believe him. For the same reasons, psychological counseling was probably not a good first choice.

Donahey would give the couple some serious penance. Besides prayers and meditation, he would prescribe work jobs around the church and the cemetery. Working together would cement their bond. Keeping them under his observation on consecrated ground for a while would be some protection in case the succubus was still in the vicinity.

Another thought occurred. He would insist they wear matching silver crosses on neck chains. He had two that had been blessed by the Pope himself. The safeguard provided should be enough to keep a rematch with the demon from occurring if they ever met again.

Two Dogs and a Pig

Father Patrick Ignatius Donahey and his blonde-haired companion stood on the back steps of the church rectory. In the yard, two black and tan dogs dodged, rolled, and caracoled in the eight inches of snow left by yesterday's January blizzard. Chunks of white stuff flew back from their paws.

Donahey squinted and said, "They look a bit large based upon my recollection of Airedales. The male must be all of fifty-five kilos."

Katherine Mary Shelly gave him a grin and a wink. "Good guess, Father. He clocks in at one hundred and twenty-five pounds. The female is twenty pounds lighter."

The dogs rose on their hind legs and pawed each other in the chest. Their breath expelled in white puffs of vapor. Falling back to all fours, the female nipped the male on his lower lip and bounded off, closely pursued.

"Kath, are these two some great experiment you're pursuing up there at the Vet lab in Ames?"

She waved a hand at the dogs, "Close, Father. We're not breeding them for size. They are Oorang Airedales, raised exclusively in the States since the early 1900's and naturally large. However, we've done some things with their genetics I can't discuss, but mainly we are working on canine-computer interface."

Donahey envisioned a cable running from a laptop to plug

into the dogs' skull. "Do they have, what do you call them, 'ports'?"

His five-foot-four companion laughed, a pleasing silvery tinkle. Kath punched his shoulder. "Oh, no. They carry a tiny computer with them. It's inserted under the baggy skin of their ruff. Bluetooth technology allows us to communicate using radio waves."

He felt a chill run through his body. "Do we have skiborgs? Are they dangerous?"

"You mean cyborgs? Well, nothing extreme. We use an iPad." She pulled a device from her jacket pocket. Kath clicked it on and swept long fingers over its surface. Little icons appeared.

She held up the nine-inch diagonal screen. "This first app allows us to track the dogs through the GPS device in their implant. We can also communicate with them in primitive ways through low wattage electrical pulses. There is a lot of additional potential to explore, but most of what we are doing is classified. This is a project funded by the Department of Defense's subdivision known as The Defense Advanced Research Projects Agency, or DARPA."

Donahey furrowed his brow and tilted his head. Computers and all their ramifications did nothing but confuse him. His life of service in the backwaters of South America left him little experienced with current techno-society. He stuffed his hands in his parka pockets as though to refuse to touch something as beyond him as rocket science. Kath caught the look and posture.

"Now, Father. You've already volunteered to keep Pal and Sal for the next two weeks while I'm at a conference. You can't back out now. Here, I'll show you, it's easy."

Father Donahey watched as she demonstrated how to turn the iPad on and off. She showed him the two icons he would need. A touch on the first one and an overhead satellite map appeared. He could recognize the church. At its rear, two little stars blinked on and off. They mimicked the dogs' play.

When activated, the other icon, shaped like a dog whistle, sent out a recall signal. Kath touched the symbol. The dogs stopped their fun and raced toward the back steps. Pal skidded to a halt and stuck his melon-sized head in Donahey's crotch. The priest jumped and pushed the head away.

"Bejiggers, I hope he doesn't do that every time."

Kath laughed and said, "He just likes you. That was an invitation to play. So, things you should know about Pal and Sal. They are three years old, which is the equivalent of twenty-eight in human years. They are excellent field dogs. Their hard-wiry outer hair allows them to slip through brush. A soft short undercoat sheds water."

"Looks like they require a lot of exercise."

"True, but you can let them run and use the recall when you've had enough." She paused to make sure the Father was paying attention. "To continue, the breed has been used to hunt big game or as family guardians. They are friendly but are fearless when aroused. They have a very high pain threshold and can take a lot of damage and still get the job done."

"Will they chase other animals? I don't want the local farmers on my back."

"Just use the recall button if they misbehave. They will stop what they are doing and return."

Donahey caught Kath looking at her watch. Her ride to the Des Moines airport was waiting. "Anything else I need to know?"

Kath frowned and waved a finger over the screen. "Father, you must promise me to use only these two icons. Do not activate the others."

Donahey gave her a wink. "I hear and obey. I hope Pal, Sal, and I will become close friends."

His companion widened her eyes. "I think you will. Teddy Roosevelt said, 'An Airedale can do anything any other dog can do and then lick the other dog, if he has to.' "

Kath kneeled and hugged the black-saddled terriers. Donahey sniffed. Pal and Sal's odor smelled like other canines he had known, a smoky, musky scent with frilly overtones of meat-based food and dog poop.

✐

Father Donahey sat in his favorite wingback chair, finishing an after-dinner coffee spiked with his favorite Templeton Rye. His canine companions lay on their individual beds, eyes drooping. A week had passed and Donahey had to admit he and the dogs were getting along much better than he had anticipated. His fellow priest and their part-time housekeeper had both laid down the law. The dogs could sleep in Donahey's office and take their meals in the kitchen, but the rest of the rectory was off limits.

The Airedales were friendly to church parishioners and neighbors, although they had treed that snooty Clara Murphy's Persian tom. The cat loved to leap out of bushes and attack the ankles of passing pedestrians. Well, it would not try that again soon. The dogs chased the cursed critter twenty feet up into a treetop. Donahey had never seen dogs leap so high.

Best of all, they enjoyed, as much as he did, long jaunts into the fields and woods of the surrounding countryside. By instinct, or training, or both, the pair would zigzag twenty to fifty feet in front of him, exploring the snowy terrain. When he turned, they raced to get in front of him again. It was good they were so attentive. Today, he had forgotten to charge the battery on the iPad and the recall signal could not be sent. However, his calls had brought them to him. The device, now plugged in, lay on the side table.

Picking it up, he studied the screen. Some nine icons arranged in three rows stared back at him. The promise not to activate the other icons was already broken. Somehow, on day one at that, he had accidentally pushed a symbol shaped like a camera when pulling the iPad out of his pocket. Two choices came up: large **X**s marked **CH1** and **CH2**. In a panic, he had touched the screen. A moving picture came up.

Snow-covered grass and bushes flashed by. A snuffling sound came from a hidden speaker. After a moment of confusion, he connected the changing pictures with the movement of Pal. A color TV camera and microphone were integrated into the dog. The picture stopped, and the camera focused on a pile of brown golf ball-sized objects. Sniffing came from the speaker. Across the bottom of the iPad a moving bar, like those on the news channels, displayed a message: **SCENT IDENTIFIED, WHITE TAIL DEER**.

"Wow!" Father Donahey said aloud. The connection to the Defense Department became clear. Among other things, these dogs were designed to be military scouts. What they saw, heard — and smelled — could be transmitted back to a handler. A patrol using these creatures would rarely be ambushed.

Pal came on point. The picture on the miniature screen froze. Centered in the screen, a male pheasant cocked its head and gave the dog a beady-eyed glare. The bar at the bottom of the screen flashed and read: Identification complete: Chinese ring-necked pheasant.

The image dissolved in a blur as the dog leaped forward. The bird exploded into the sky. Donahey looked up in time to see the sun catch the iridescent copper, green, and red of the cock's breast, head, and wing feathers. The sight never failed to make him catch his breath, the bird caught in a moment of exquisite beauty. Sal and Pal pursued. The pheasant dropped into the cornrows of an adjacent field. Donahey didn't think the dogs would catch it. The bird would land, dodge left or right, and run as fast as a horse.

After much fumbling, the priest had managed to reset the device by shutting it off and turning it on. He hit the recall and the trio ambled home.

Donahey took another sip of coffee. He studied the other symbols. One was shaped as a globe with tiny continents, obviously the earth. The craving came over him to explore. He felt guilty. Oh, well, he thought, in for a penny, in for a pound. He had already taken a risk with the camera icon, might as well go all the way. Tapping the sphere brought up a small numerical keypad and a drop-down menu of two items: **GO TO** and **RETURN**. Touching **GO TO** produced two boxes labeled: **LAT** and **LONG**.

His mind leaped. Entering a series of latitude and longitude coordinates would allow the computer to direct the dogs to specific locations. He envisioned them scouting enemy positions or packing fifteen to twenty pounds of supplies to friendly troops.

He returned the screen to the start point. Two other icons appeared to be programmed. One was a Red Cross, or first aid symbol, and the other — a rifle with a bayonet. Donahey looked at the two dogs slumped on their beds. Both relaxed after exercise and a good meal. Their eyes drooped in half-sleep. He raised a finger. His heart began to beat faster. A touch on the rifle icon and a safety question came up:

ACTIVATE ATTACK MODE? >YES >NO

Suddenly alert, Pal and Sal's heads popped up. Eyes opened wide. Ears went flat against their heads. Two-inch claws extended, cat-like, from their toes. Lips pulled back. Jaws opened, exposing rows of finger-sized pointed teeth. For a moment, he thought he was looking into alligator mouths. The animals appeared to have bigger and more than the usual number of teeth. Donahey shuddered and stabbed the iPad off button. Claws retracted, mouths closed. The dogs relaxed and lay back.

Father Donahey's bottom felt tingly from sitting too long on the rough bark of a long-fallen walnut tree. The two dogs sat in front of him, ears up and reddish-pink tongues hanging out the sides of their mouths. The combination of quivering bodies and excited facial expressions sent a message — one begging to be released to run and explore.

For their outing today, he had borrowed the Church's old rattletrap 1956 Ford F-100 pickup. The faded red vehicle had rusted out door panels and blossoming oxidation spots on its chrome, but it started every day, huffing and puffing oily bluish-gray breath. Eight years its elder, Donahey felt sympathy for the aged vehicle. He and the truck both needed new parts and a cosmetic work over.

Man and dogs side-by-side in the cab had traveled five miles south from Winterset on Millstream Avenue to Clanton Creek Recreational Area. The park's one-thousand-plus acres were kept pristine, with only pedestrian traffic allowed in its combination of woods, savannah, and tall-grass prairie.

"Shake," he commanded.

Pal lifted his right paw. Donahey's fingers squeezed the flesh surrounding the middle toe. A silvery looking spike two inches long pushed out. He ran his thumb across its edge. "Ouch," he exclaimed. A thin line of blood appeared on the skin of the digit. The talon, or whatever it might be, was sharper than the blades of his favorite multi-bladed stockman's knife.

He raised the paw closer to his sixty-seven-year-old eyes. In circumference, it was as wide and long as his own hand. Webbing between the toes made for a good swimmer and would help support the animal's weight on snow. He wondered again exactly how the canines would be used. His sense of ethics rebelled at the thought of them being used in warfare. Yet, dogs had probably been the first creatures to be suborned by men. If humans must kill and destroy, let them do it to themselves, and leave God's other creations in peace.

Pal and Sal's ears snapped to attention, their heads cocked and turned left. Donahey held his breath. The forest had grown quiet. The sound of squabbling bluejays and the flutter of bird wings had ceased. Bright sunlight had brought out flocks and pairs of chickadees, pine juncos, and goldfinches, the latter now dressed in white-striped black wings and winter olive. He shivered and noticed that clouds had moved in to obscure the sun. Shadows, which had clearly delineated the shape of each individual tree, were gone now. The resulting gray-gloom transformed the forest into a one-dimensional charcoal rendering.

The crack of a breaking twig pulled his head at the same angle as the Airedales. Donahey strained eyes and ears. The dogs leaped over the log, passing one on each side of the priest. Surprised, he fell backward, landing on his back in the snow.

Pal and Sal began to bark. A human voice shouted and yelled. Legs still up on the trunk, Father Donahey wiggled and squirmed. His thrashing arms left the swirl patterns of a half snow angel. Using his arms to free one leg and then the other, he managed to roll over and regain his feet. About three trees deeper into the forest, the dogs circled a shadowy figure with its back up against a trunk. Donahey rushed forward, booted feet sinking into drifted snow with each step.

He skidded to a halt, slipping on ice hidden under its white cover. Donahey caught sight of short cut black hair — the man had lost his hat. The dogs bounded in and out. Dressed in Carhartt brown bib overhauls and quilted cotton duck work jacket, the stranger thrust and swung at them with an exotic weapon. What looked like a combination spear and axe heads had been fixed to a ten-foot wooden shaft. Recognition flooded his mind.

"Jimmy. Jimmy Wong, what are you doing?"

The man glanced at the priest and grimaced. He shook the weapon. "Father, call off your dogs!"

Donahey fumble-fingered the iPad. He managed to get it clicked on and punched the **RECALL** button. Pal and Sal rushed to his side. Jimmy lifted his weapon to the vertical and approached.

The priest's memory supplied background information. The Wong family had been members of the church since the late 1930s. Jimmy's grandfather had immigrated to Winterset with Catholic missionaries to escape the Japanese invasion of China. The various generations since had farmed three hundred acres adjacent to this park. The locals, with what had initially been a racist reaction, labeled the spread the Wrong Farm. The name had stuck, but it was like calling a bald man Curly or a tall man Shorty. The Wongs were the top-rated farmers of the area. Their crops always achieved the highest yields while losing mere fractions of topsoil.

"Well, Father, I did not expect to see you," he waved a hand towards the dogs, "and your companions out here today."

"I know they allow black powder, bow, and shotgun hunting in these woods, but is there a spear season I don't know about?"

Jimmy blushed, his already tan cheeks and forehead darkening further. He shook the weapon. "Not a spear, Father. It's a *ji*."

"Come, let's sit and talk, my son."

Seated together on the walnut log, the pair shared a plastic bottle of Fiji water. Donahey prepared and lit his pipe. The dogs sat nearby. He let the silence grow. Many years listening to confessions told him the truth would only come if his parishioners spoke first. Asking questions would not get to the heart of the matter.

Jimmy looked around. He propped the *ji* against the tree trunk. His hands went to cover his face. In a muffled voice, he spoke. "Father, I need help. I am desperate. It's my daughter, Lien."

Donahey remembered Jimmy was a widower; his wife had died in childbirth twenty-five years ago. The girl baby had survived and grew to be a fine figure of a lass. She had made the varsity cross country teams in high school and at the university, graduated valedictorian. He hadn't seen Lien recently. Her reporting job with National Public Radio kept her flying from one national and international news event to another.

He fished for more information. "I heard she was back visiting."

Jimmy clasped his hands together and pressed them against his lips. "You are one of the few who might just believe me if I say Lien is possessed by an evil spirit."

Donahey looked at his companion and the spear-axe at his side. A horrible feeling welled up. "You are surely not going to use that... that *ji* on your daughter?

Jimmy's head jerked up, "No, Father, heaven forbid. You must help. Let me tell you what happened."

"As you might suspect, my son, I am a good listener." He sucked on the pipe. It had gone out. Donahey pulled an old-fashioned wooden kitchen match from a side pocket of his parka and struck it into flame against the log's surface.

"In spite of the Japanese War and the later communist government, our family has always managed to visit our relatives in China. Lien returned from such a visit a month ago. In the old days, the family farmed in Guangdong Province. When the communists began the new open economic policy, the province grew dramatically in both manufacturing and population. All the old village ways were lost.

"Factories, highways, and apartments were constructed on thousands of acres of land. What wasn't covered with concrete was poisoned with toxic industrial chemicals from unregulated dumping. The destruction and pressures of growth forced spirits and demons off lands they had inhabited for thousands of years. Priests were no longer able to placate and contain the nastiest ones.

'Wraiths and fiends are migrating, attempting to find new homes. They take possession of human bodies in order to travel."

Father Donahey placed a hand on Jimmy's back. "And how do you know Lien brought one back from her trip?"

"All the signs indicate the presence of the demon *Zhu Bajie*. In the long, long ago, he lived in heaven. Drink and lust led him to attack the beautiful Moon Goddess. When she complained, the Jade Emperor threw him down to earth to live as a human. Unfortunately, he fell into a pig pen and was reborn as a man-eating pig demon."

"How can you be sure this is the one?"

"The pig personality manifests greed in everything: eating, drinking, and pleasures of the flesh. My daughter has gained thirty pounds in the last month. Her appetite for alcoholic drink, drugs, and sex is off the chart."

"Jimmy, I will call the Bishop. We can get exorcists."

"By the time they get here it will be too late, Father. As *Zhu* becomes more entrenched, his aura will affect everything for miles. Can you imagine the entire population of Winterset engaging in one massive orgy around the town square?"

"Where is Lien now?" Donahey scanned the woods around them. "Is she here in the woods?"

"At the moment, she is safe. Using Skype and the Internet, I consulted with demon-chasers in the old country." Jimmy pulled a rolled-up leather bag from inside his jacket and handed it to Donahey. "They gave me directions on how to make the *ji* and this magic bag to contain the evil one's *chi*."

The ivory-colored material of the bag felt soft and leathery to Donahey's fingers. The outside was completely covered with mystical Chinese characters. "I don't understand."

"In a multiple Skype, we chanted words from ancient holy books to force the demon out of Lien's body. I held the bag over her mouth and nostrils. The chants would drive *Zhu's* spirit out into the container. The bag containing the wraith would then be air-freighted back to China, where it would be locked away."

Donahey removed the pipe and rubbed his chin. "And, it apparently didn't work."

Jimmy moaned and rocked. "I blew it, Father. The demon left her body. The bag slipped, and it escaped. With the chanting, it couldn't immediately go back into Lien. It broke out into the barnyard and possessed my prize Yorkshire boar. It's now roaming these woods."

This was new territory to Donahey. He had only participated in one exorcism. That 'casting out' had been handled by a professional. It had only been a lower grade spirit putting up little resistance. "So, what are you hoping to do now?"

"The elders told me, I must find and disable the creature enough to allow the bag to be secured around its muzzle." He shook the spear-axe. "Then I will kill it. When the body dies, *Zhu* must leave and be contained. Can you and your dogs help?"

Father Donahey brought a hand to his lips; brows came together. Staring into the woods, he twisted the bag in his hands. He tried to imagine the threat to his parishioners and to the population of the entire area. A vision of nude bodies writhing in heaps on the courthouse lawn came to his mind like a Hieronymus Bosch medieval painting of souls being tortured in hell.

The viewpoint in his hallucination changed, swooped lower, stopping at ground level next to one locked together couple. It was he, naked and straining on top of Clara Murphy. Skinny age-spotted arms pulled him tight against her pillow-sized breasts. Her legs locked around his thighs.

And, somewhere among that moaning, giggling tangle of Iowans the pig-god was selecting a human for its next meal. No, it must not be! He... we must stop it.

Donahey wiped sweat from his forehead. "Jimmy, the three of us will help."

Maybe it was no coincidence he and the dogs happened to be in the right place at the right time. He pointed at the ancient pattern pole weapon. "Don't you have a rifle or shotgun we could use?"

"Lead won't damage it," Jimmy raised the *ji*, "only enchanted cold iron." He locked eyes with Donahey. "It will be very dangerous, Father. *Zhu* will resist. He will try to kill and eat us."

⟋

The hunting party picked up the split-hoofed prints of the

boar in the new snow. The dogs bounded ahead, following the scent. Even the humans' diminished noses could smell the sulfur rotten egg manure odor left by the demon's corporal body. The two men struggled to keep up.

Pal and Sal vanished from sight. Donahey pulled out the iPad and turned on the GPS tracking. The two stars marking the animals' positions curved through the woods. The trace they followed ran in a circle. He motioned to Jimmy. They cut through the woods in a diagonal to intercept the dogs and their prey.

The Airedales let out high-pitched warbling, half-growls, half-whines. A sharp porcine shriek followed, loud enough to make the humans' ears hurt. The pair of hunters broke out of the trees into a small clearing.

The eight-hundred-pound boar squealed and chomped his tushes. Its rear end pushed safely back into a brush pile, it faced outward snapping and hooking eight-inch long curled tusks at its tormentors. Pal and Sal raced back and forth keeping the boar locked in place.

Jimmy shouted, "Christ Almighty! Father, forgive me for those words, but that demon has transformed my boar."

Donahey looked closer. Six-inch long prickly bristles covered every square inch of its black-mottled skin. The head and body were leaner and bonier. And no domestic boar had tusks that long. It looked like a slapped together combination of all the nastiest features of African warthog, Arkansas razorback, and Siberian wild boar. Sunken in flaps of fat, its tiny piggy eyes glared at the men and dogs. In the gray gloom, they glowed blood red.

Lines from Shakespeare's *Venus and Adonis* came to Donahey's mind.

> *His eyes like glow-worms shine when he doth fret;*
> *His snout digs sepulchers where 'er he goes.*

"Father, we need to get it out in the open, so I can get a whack at it. You and the dogs keep its attention. I'll sneak around the back and give it a poke."

"Wait a minute." Donahey commanded. He grasped his pocket cross in one hand and the haft of the *ji* in the other. "Our Father in Heaven, please bless our effort. If it is your will, give us success in defeating this denizen of Hell. Amen." He released the spear-axe and drew the sign of the cross on its metal. *"In Nomine Patris, et Filii, et Spiritus Sancti."*

An aura of rainbow-colored energy, St. Elmo's fire, enveloped the metal of the polearm. A combination of heathen ancient Chinese and Christian blessings now powered the weapon. Jimmy hustled off. Father Donahey advanced to distract the beast. He waved the bag and shouted. Emboldened by his presence, the dogs rushed in both at once to snap and dance.

He heard a shout from behind the brush pile. "Here it comes!"

The massive boar squealed and exploded out. A twelve-inch long spear point in the anus was too much, even for a demon. Pig snout in his crotch, Donahey was lifted and tossed backward like a rag doll. He hit the brush pile and bounced off to land on his face. He pushed himself up. He felt a stinging sensation — the boar had gored him on his inner right leg. Adrenaline flooded his bloodstream. The dogs and the boar roared and howled. Their zigzagging, weaving bodies became an intricate dance of death. He must give the Airedales every advantage.

Donahey pulled out the iPad, touched the rifle icon and then the **YES** button. Pal and Sal became blurs. Long slashes appeared on the sides of the pig. Blood squirted out. Sal zipped in. A terrible high-pitched squeal came out. She danced back out of tusk range. The dog shook her head, tossing a pig ear and a strip of neck skin to one side. The two Airedales dove in again. The action froze.

Pal had *Zhu's* back leg clamped in his jaws. Sal had a grip on the pig's jowl on the opposite side. They held their quivering prey still. Donahey limped forward and thrust the bag over the slobbering piggy mouth and flat-nosed nostrils. Jimmy appeared in his side vision, the *ji* raised over his head. The sickle-shaped axe portion came down. In amateur hands, the razor-sharp blade hit at an angle. The axe head bounced off the pig's skull shearing off a flap of skin four inches wide and eight inches long.

The boar reacted. It shook off the dogs. The bag slipped from Donahey's grasp, exposing snot-covered nose holes. The axe came down again. The fine-honed cold iron found the spine where it joined the skull and chopped it in two.

A brown mist blew out of the boar's snout and burned into Father Donahey's mouth. It tasted like shit. He fell back. Inside him, the demon-spirit and his priest's soul struggled. He saw Jimmy's distorted face bend over him.

"Father, oh God. Not you too?"

He sat up. Everything was tinted red. He tried to stand and then fell back. His right leg wouldn't work. Adrenalin had masked the pain of a long tusk slash on the inside of his thigh. It had bled, soaking his pant leg. Liquid squished in his boot. In a dream state, he held up the iPad and pushed the Red Cross icon. Sal pushed her face in and began to lick the wound. The iPad dropped into the snow. A sudden bout of dizziness felt alien. He shuddered and let out a long series of pig-grunts.

Feelings and emotions coalesced. The demon personality took control. A ferocious, hungry emptiness welled up. The pig-man began to get an erection. Its head spun around. A three-point crawl took the creature to the boar carcass. The new *Zhu* began to feed. Jimmy smacked it in the ribs with the pole-arm haft. Head turned. Jaws slobbered. Teeth nipped. Eyes glowed red.

Huddled in a tiny sliver of his repressed humanity, Donahey heard Jimmy say, "Forgive me, Father." The flat part of the axe came down on his head.

❧

The Donahey-*Zhu* creature woke. Hunger and the desire

to kill filled him to bursting. All of the Seven Deadly Sins —
lust, gluttony, greed, sloth, wrath, envy, and pride — raged
and fought inside its bloated sack of skin. It tried to rise. The
hybrid was secured to a bed by sticky silvery bandages. Flex-
ing the body caused the frame to bounce – a random atonal
drumbeat against the hardwood floor. The demon roared. The
sound was muffled. Someone had secured a bag over its nose
and mouth. It tossed its head, trying to dislodge the suffocating sack. No luck. It was stuck on with more of the silver tape.

The sound of group chanting from a computer speaker cut
through its anger. They wanted it to come out. *No, nooo! Not
again to be confined*. The pig-god bucked. Hands and feet
quivered. Fingers and toes clasped and unclasped. Faster and
faster. The crusted scab on the thigh wound cracked. Blood
flowed. Bits of demon personality dissolved and floated out
through nostrils and mouth. The priest personality inside began to pray. It was too much.

☙

Donahey lay propped up on Jimmy's bed, lips in a weak
smile. An EMT worked on his leg. Sheriff Rick sat in a bentwood rocker, drinking coffee from a brightly colored Beijing
Olympics souvenir mug. Jimmy sat, tight-lipped, in a spoke-
backed Windsor chair brought in from the kitchen. Pal and Sal
lay in the space between the two men, heads on crossed paws.

The med-tech spoke, "Father, I've finished stitching. Looks
like someone stopped the bleeding and sterilized the wound.
It's as clean as can be. Not sure how that could have happened.
At any rate have your doc check it out tomorrow."

Lien walked in bearing a tray of chocolate chip cookies. She
winked at the priest and provided a cover story. "We used Chinese medicine."

Donahey thought, "And having genetically modified dogs
who have coagulants and antibiotics in their saliva helps
immensely."

The tech took two cookies in passing and left the house. The room was silent until they heard the ambulance pull away, its tires crackling ice-coated gravel on the driveway.

The rocker creaked as the sheriff leaned forward. "Okay, I need to file a report. Let me get the story straight. Father, you were out exercising the dogs when you came upon Jimmy looking for his escaped boar. You decided to help him. When you two and the dogs finally cornered the pig, it went wild and attacked. Father Donahey was injured. Jimmy, you were forced to kill it."

"That's right, Sheriff. The good Father was unconscious. I cut down two saplings and made a *travois* for the dogs to pull. Got him back to the house and called for help"

"Well, that all sounds good, except for a few strange odds and ends. For example, the boar was almost decapitated with a sharp heavy object. I'd guess an axe of some kind. Why an axe when a gun would kill from a distance and no one hurt?"

Rick pushed his Stetson to the back of his head. "Someone fed on the raw carcass. Bite marks looked like they were made with human teeth. And, we have one hell of a bump on the Father's head. A fact not consistent with the story."

Jimmy began to wiggle in his chair. Sweat beads appeared on his forehead.

The sheriff also has a secret, Donahey thought. He recalled the killing of two escaped criminals by the sheriff's alter ego, an Irish shape-shifting pooka. He needed to talk to the sheriff alone. "Jimmy, fetch the poleaxe. Lien, could you get me a cup of that coffee? Smells great."

The priest waited until father and daughter had left the room. "Rick, I don't think you want to pursue this any further. Please accept my assurances that this episode is closed and there will be no further danger to anyone."

"Father, I have my duty."

"I know, my son. But you are in an excellent position to understand, as someone who has one foot in the mundane world and one in the supernatural."

Jimmy returned with the bloodied *ji*. Sheriff Rick's eyes grew wide. He sniffed. The arteries in his neck pulsed. Jimmy handed him the weapon. It almost slipped from his hand. The sheriff raised one finger and touched the blade. He jerked it back and stuck it in his mouth.

The lawman scrutinized the two men's faces. His eyebrows, cheeks, and lips relaxed. He stroked his chin. "I think I should dispose of this. It's probably illegal under Iowa law."

Father Donahey leaned back, let out his breath, and relaxed tense muscles. The sheriff had yielded to his gentle blackmail.

Donahey said, "Any further questions, Sheriff?" He caught a micro-expression. For the briefest of seconds, the sheriff's face flashed black. In his eyes, frozen demon fire flared.

"No. I think this file is best closed." He forced a smile. "In this case, two Wongs make a right."

Donahey's brow wrinkled and he rolled his eyes. It was a groaner. So far, except for the leprechaun, supernatural creatures had lacked even a modicum of human-style humor.

Sheriff Rick rose from the rocker. "I'll be on my way. I think I'll set up a speed trap over on east highway 92."

He nodded to Jimmy and Lien. "I always feel better after nailing a few DWIs."

Donahey blew on the coffee and took a sip. He noticed his pipe and the iPad on the bedside table.

Lien smiled and said, "Father, will you join us for dinner? We're going to have pork chops."

His stomach was still extended from the demon-forced meal in the woods. The memory made a tablespoon of vomit flutter up his esophagus. Lips squeezed together. He gulped and swallowed. "No thanks, Lien. I don't think I have it in me to ever eat pork again."

Fire and Water

Sparks swirled skyward. Father Donahey tried to find patterns as fiery motes and black feathery ash twisted and writhed against a dark sky. Typical, he thought, the human mind always trying to pigeonhole and categorize nature. The fire popped and sputtered. It consumed a mix of last year's corncobs and dead, dry branches. The wood portion of the fuel came from a hundred-year-old three-row-thick windbreak of interlocked cedar, spruce, and pine trees. Rabbits, a badger, and birds galore had made it home.

This living barrier of plants and animals surrounded and protected the ramshackle two-story house to their rear. Once the five-generation home of an Iowa farm family, the gray-weathered structure was now a dormitory for migrant laborers.

The 1930s Craftsman style building was barely habitable, with no working heat or air conditioning. The oak window frames had shrunk, allowing prairie wind and dust to pass through without hindrance. Near the broken-backed front porch, an old iron faucet fixed to a three-foot high vertical pipe supplied water provided by the rural water district. No connection to the house meant the inhabitants needed to use outhouses and galvanized tubs out back for washing clothes and bodies.

The interior had the smell of musty rotting boards, dead

mice, sweaty humans, and jalapeno and poblano peppers. On the plus side, some of the electrical outlets still worked, which allowed cooking, refrigeration, and radio and CD playing. As proof, music drifted out through the ratty screen door. Donahey hummed along with Maria Grever's classic song *Júrame*, sung by tenor José Mojica.

Bésame
Con un beso enamorado
Como nadie me ha besado
Desde el día en que nací.

The song ended too soon, replaced by popular mariachi selections. Donahey sat back and let the blending of violin, *vihuela*, guitar, *guitarrón*, and trumpet relax him.

In the chair to his left, accompanied by a familiar brown face, the priest felt a relaxation he had not experienced since retiring to the small Iowa town of Winterset. The soft vowels and rolled rs of New World Spanish were a comfort to his ears. His forty-five years of service in various South American countries had made it difficult to feel at home in the local sea of white faces and harsh Anglo-Saxon consonants.

Burned-through branches in the fire collapsed, puffing out a cloud of sparks. Donahey brushed glowing embers off his pant legs. He didn't want holes charred into his priest's wool-polyester blend black trousers. He and Adelita, a Mexicana woman with gray-streaked raven-hued hair, sat in beat up aluminum-framed lawn chairs. Two empty chairs awaited additional arrivals. Who might be coming he didn't know. An agitated Adelita had requested his presence. Her explanation was full of strange words and phrases, neither English nor Spanish. He gradually picked out that there was to be a meeting and it had something to do with the strange weather.

The fire had been built more for sociability than the need for warmth. God knows they didn't need any more heat. Since the spring equinox in March, the climate had been unseasonably hot and dry. Temperatures in the high nineties combined with lack of rain had blasted Madison County. The unusual weather was localized to an astounding extent. According to crop reports on the radio, the corn and soybeans in the rest of the state had received the usual amount of precipitation and were progressing normally.

Good enough subsoil moisture left over from fall and winter rains had allowed the county's May-planted seeds to sprout and spread fragile leaves. In June, area farmers expected an average of four and a half inches of rain and temperatures not to exceed eighty degrees. The combination of drought and excessive temperatures stunted plants that should have reached fifty centimeters or twenty inches high by this time.

Given his past experience with the supernatural, Father Donahey had begun to suspect the area was suffering under the curse of a supernatural creature. There must be something special about this patch of earth. Not quite a year had passed since his arrival, and he had already been a spectator or participant in adventures involving an Irish shape-shifting wraith, a succubus/incubus, a leprechaun, and the Chinese pig-god *Zhu Bajie*. Before each one, he had experienced an itchy, prickly, tickly sort of feeling, both mentally and physically.

All this had led him to this old house and to these folks. Like many rural places in the country, migrant labor had become a necessity. With it came all the problems of an established population rubbing up against a flow of newcomers bringing with them a vibrant different culture. The country was in the disruptive process of value clash and the prejudice of the old ruling class. It would pass, but in the meantime they had to deal with the nastier aspects. His companion spoke.

"Padre, gracias por toda su ayuda con la litigo."

"Adelita, de nada, el juez falló en contra de nosotros."

He didn't agree that she should thank him. They had only won part of the court case. A large seed company had leased several thousand acres of cropland. The corporation had hired a contractor to provide immigrant labor to detassel and sort hybrid corn. The El Camino Real Company owned by Ricardo and Josefina Lopez had taken the money and recruited Mexican labor.

The workers had been treated badly. They came to Father Donahey for help. Adelita, who spoke the least-fractured English, had been elected to represent the workers. Normally quiet and in her late forties, the woman had turned into a tough, stubborn advocate for her fellows. Her short stature — four feet four, thin gray hair, and back problems from too many years of stoop labor — presented no obstacles to her determination.

A proponent of liberation theology, Donahey believed two components formed a priest's duty. Besides preparing the poor and repressed for treasures in heaven, the Church should help them achieve a modicum of justice and comfort in this world. He had compiled a long list of violations of the Iowa Agricultural Workers Act. Wages had not been paid when due, illegal deductions had been made, housing was inadequate, and pay stubs had not been provided to show hours worked. Required drinking water and porta-potties had not been provided in the fields.

Donahey had led the effort to bring a civil suit in court. The final ruling had let the big corporation off the hook, since it had made all required payments to the contractor. The judge ruled against the contractors. However, the Lopezes had disappeared and no money could be recovered. The next month, the drought and heat began.

The radio cut out in the middle of a smooth baritone voice announcing the next song. A long rumbling sputter-cough resembling a big cat at hunt came from the road. The single headlight of a motorcycle flickered and jerked as its tires bounced and jounced in the rutted lane leading up to the house.

The bike spun up around the fire, its rear tire sliding across the dead brown grass. A wave of exhaust fumes and powdery soil swirled up to form a miniature dust devil. The fire flared up — light, no heat — illuminating a surreal sight. Donahey blinked and shook his head. The riders, a man and a woman, stared.

The driver wore a black leather vest with gold-rayed Aztec sun symbols embossed on the sides. Jeans, tight against the hips, blossomed out above the ankles to engulf leather boots crossed with buckled straps with carved silver jaguar heads. Nine-inch long wristbands, a skull-cap of black leather, and aviator style sunglasses completed his costume.

His companion raised her chin, pushed out her chest, and leaned back languidly. Black hair hung down her back, pulled tight and woven into a single centered braid. A silver squash blossom necklace rested on top of a sleeveless peasant blouse. Armbands of black volcanic glass set in raw silver bands matched similar bracelets on her wrists. She slid off the back of the bike. Donahey noticed the quiver of breasts not bound by a bra. Both outfits and the bike were dulled with gray-black powder from the road.

Eyebrows up in surprise, Donahey examined the machine they straddled. A basic Harley low rider of indeterminate age had been highly customized. It was painted flat black everywhere, except... His facial expression became one of horror, it appeared as though human bones had been integrated into the mechanism.

An open-jawed skull enclosed the headlight, and the neck vertebrae extended back to where clavicles joined the frame. The spine and rib cage encompassed the tank and the space under the rider's seat. The passenger appeared to sit on the pelvis. From the thing's shoulders, clean-picked humerus, ulna, and radius of the arms followed the curves of the handlebars. The metacarpals and phalanges of the fingers wrapped around the end grips. When the driver twisted the grip-throttle, it looked like he was shaking a skeletal hand. The legs bent back at the hips and knees to follow the curves of the rear cowl.

The fire died down and Father Donahey could see the bones

phosphoresce — they had been painted with a compound to glow in the dark. He imagined the flat-black Harley racing at night, the skeleton afire, looking like a prone carcass flying three feet above the highway with its arms extended, waiting to scoop up victims.

Yet, there was something wrong. He gripped the arms of his chair and leaned forward. His mind struggled to reconstruct the full-body chart they had used many years ago in the Jesuit anatomy class at the university. The bones were impossible — much larger than normal, and too many ribs. The pelvic spread resembled that of a woman, but the shoulders would be massive. The arms and legs were too long and the neck too short for either gender. The whole thing was bogus. Donahey leaned back in his chair and relaxed.

The woman rider picked up on his disbelief and smiled. "You are right, Father. Teco had a sculptor friend of his make the bones. They are not proportioned right, *verdad*?" She glanced at her companion, her head shook slightly, and lips upturned. "In his mind, he is not *espantoso...* scary enough without resorting to tricks."

The man swatted her on the rear and replied "Ah, Patli, *mi corazón*, you liked my tricks well enough last night."

The pair stretched arms, rolled shoulders, and paced, their legs slightly bowed from too long in the saddle. Donahey took the time to closely examine the two. Both were short by U.S. standards. The man, he guessed, at five feet four and the woman some ten inches shorter. Teco removed his helmet and ran fingers through long black hair. A scraggly, thin mustache formed a single straight line across the upper lip. Stocky, not much waist there, the large well-muscled chest appeared to be fixed directly to his hips.

Both the man and the woman shared aquiline noses. Both pairs of eyes had the typical epicanthic fold inherited from ancestors that had walked or boated across the Bering Strait thirty thousand years ago. As usual, it was difficult to tell their ages. Youthful, he thought, but they moved with an assurance only achieved by experience and maturity. Another glance at Patli and, except for the nose, he saw the singer and actor Cher. In fact, the couple resembled Sonny and Cher in their middle years.

Donahey raised one eyebrow as he noticed the way their bodies exerted a magnetic attraction for each other. He had seen lovers in the thousands during his many years in the priesthood. The delicate dance of attraction gave away their knowing intimacy — the bodies signaled their compulsion for each other.

*

He remembered his own indiscretion. Just turned sixteen, he forked hay into the age-blackened manger in his family's thatchroofed, stonewalled barn. Old Molly, a speckled brown on white Irish Moiled milk cow, trotted up to take her breakfast. A familiar female voice made the hackles of his neck stand up.

"Suren, yer getting more hay into the mud than into the cow."

The bane of his life, Fiona Molloy, had come to ruin his day, even before they met on their way to school. She constantly butted into his life to tease and criticize. His grandfather had warned him about redheads like her.

"Blondes are wild, brunettes are true, but ya never know what a redhead will do."

Donahey turned, irritated. "Fiona, can ye not give me a little peace..."

The girl was only inches away. His eyebrows, head, and shoulders lifted, arms came up as if to push her away. She moved in between them, making body contact. Her flesh was warm against the coolness emanating from the stone walls. Fiona's freckled hands removed her shawl. She shook out long auburn hair. A lock fell across one eye.

Donahey started to speak. She placed one long finger across

his lips and whispered "shhhh" — the sibilants strangely arousing. Her arms enveloped him and squeezed so tightly his ribs popped. He couldn't tell whether it was her strength or his confusion that made him breathless. From a primitive portion of his brain came the knowledge of what might be happening. Fiona felt his body tense. She placed a bare foot behind his ankle and pushed. They fell into the sweet-smelling dry grasses. Old Molly continued to munch, her liquid brown eyes wise, as she watched.

Donahey blinked. He blessed Fiona's memory. It was just the one time, but it had made him more human and added an experience which allowed him empathy for his parishioners. That all-too-human desire was the root of much that was good and bad. A man or woman could easily be led into strange places and relationships by the organs of regeneration.

Adelita grasped his forearm, "Father, these are Tecocol and Patli. They understand what has happened here, and can restore our situation before the land changes into a permanent desert."

Teco and Patli slumped into the empty lawn chairs. "My mouth feels like *ratones pequeños* have made a nest. Anything to drink?"

Adelita reached to her side and slid the lid off a cooler. She popped the tops off sweating bottles of Mexican Bohemia beer and passed one to each of the new arrivals and one to Donahey. Bottles lifted in unison.

In three swallows, Teco emptied half the contents. He turned to Donahey, smiled, and waved the bottle. "That was as welcome as a mother's kiss." Stretching his legs out and crossing them, he stared into the fire and began to talk.

"*Jefe*, you have a mess. Some of the *compañeros* that worked here got bad advice — and action — from an aficionado, a dabbler, an... as you say, an amateur. This one has... *estar uno muy pagado de sí mismo*." Teco searched for a translation.

Patli responded, "He means one who has a great and undeserved opinion of himself."

Teco grasped her hand and brought it to his lips for a kiss. "*Gracias.* Anyway, this *cabrón* knew enough to invoke the old gods to punish the folks who cheated his clients. The *idiota* brought down their wraith on Madison County, cursing the innocent while the Lopezes escaped."

Father Donahey broke in, "*Mi hijo*, can we ask this *brujo* to release the curse?"

"That would be the easy way. But *el Bobo* does not know how to do that. So now we have a *chingao* situation — all fucked up."

Donahey blushed and pursed his lips. "Exactly what are we facing?"

Teco glanced at Patli, then tilted his head and raised his eyebrows.

She crossed her ankles and took a sip of beer. "*Padre*, this is a story from the old days of death and rebirth.

"At the beginning of time there came into being four gods: *Huitzilopochtli, Tezcatlipoca, Xipe Totec*, and *Quetzalcoatl*. They created all other things. *Tezcatlipoca* created the sun, a new source of power. *Quetzalcoatl* became jealous and in a fight with *Tezcatlipoca* destroyed the first sun. The *Coatl* birthed a new *sol* and as an afterthought created humans.

"In time a third sun evolved; *Tlaloc*, the god of rain and water took over the burden of warming the earth. *Tezcatlipoca*, still suffering from hurt pride, hounded *Tlaloc* night and day, even killing some of his children. The grief-stricken god's heart poured out fire and withheld the rain. The sun swelled until it self-destructed and was replaced by a fourth *sol*.

"*Padre*, we currently live under the fifth sun. The false *brujo* has brought back the third sun. He is now unable to control it or send it back to the past."

"*Mi hija*, what is the answer? Do we wait until it destroys itself?"

Patli waved her beer. "No good, Father. The gods' time is different than ours. It may be ages until the resurrected Tlaloc gives it up. And then there will be no sun, only darkness and cold beyond imagining."

Donahey shifted in his chair. "Adelita has asked me here at your request. What do you need from me?"

Teco leaned forward and spoke, "We have a plan. It will all happen tomorrow at midnight, when the Lopezes, you, and we come together."

"But the Lopezes are in Mexico."

Teco smiled and turned to Patli. "Tell *el Jefe* where the bad guys are."

Patli stood and squinted her eyes. She turned, an arm lifted, and she pointed southwest. "They are on I-35, nearing Oklahoma City. It is likely they will spend the night there."

Donahey frowned. Teco caught the expression. "She always knows where the enemy is. Patli is a *profeta*, a... a..."

Adelita translated, "She is a diviner, a fortune teller, a seer."

The priest sat back and grimaced. "Is there some proof?"

Patli smiled, bright even teeth reflected the firelight. Teco laughed. "Well, *Jefe*, she can go deeper and tell your true fortune, but you must provide the trigger." He slapped his knee and broke into raucous laughter at the thought. "You must bring her to *orgasmo*. Only at the height of *trato sexual* do the gods give her power."

Donahey blushed. "Not going to happen. All right, say I accept her foretelling. Why would the Lopezes return to the scene of the crime, where they might be arrested?"

Adelita spoke, "Father, you can only take $10,000 in currency across the Mexican border. The Lopezes could not open a bank account since the court ruling would impound their publicly known assets. So no bank transfers could be ordered or even ATM withdrawals done, across the border. They hid the majority of their loot, close to two hundred thousand dollars, here."

"*Sí, Jefe*," Patli said, "I have foretold it. They will be at this house tomorrow night to recover the *dinero*. And, so will the four of us. At that time Teco and I will perform our ritual, justice will happen, and *el sol* will return to normal."

Donahey hunched his shoulders; he felt the itchy-tingly feeling spread throughout his body. "What part will I play in all this?"

"We will be appealing to *Xipe Totec*, the god of the seasons, renewal, and growing things. From the spring equinox to summer is his time of year. This resurrection and its destruction is a slap in his face."

The feeling of foreboding grew stronger. The priest's hands began to shake. He repeated, "And what part am I to play?"

Patli's cool fingers caressed the hair on his right forearm. She whispered, "You are the *salvaguardia, o el* plan B."

"The old gods," Teco said, "are unpredictable. If they refuse to release us, you must force them to let us go. In the old days, the Christian gods and the Aztec gods warred. The Christian gods brought by Cortez won. As a priest of the victors you have power over them."

"What Christian gods?"

"*¡Hijole!* The Father, the Son, the Holy Ghost, Virgin Mary, St. Joseph, and all the other saints and martyrs. Don't you know your own religion?"

Donahey shook his head, rolled his eyes, and decided this was not the time for a lesson in Christianity.

"All right, I'll be here at midnight tomorrow with my stole, Bible, holy water, and cross."

"Remember, you do nothing unless we get into trouble."

Donahey huffed and puffed. He stood upright and pumped the pedals of the church's old balloon-tired Schwinn. Sweat poured off the priest's forehead and stung his eyes. His watch read 12:45 and he was late.

His primary transportation, a 1956 Ford 100 pickup, had

developed a case of the vapors at the last minute. Weakening twin circles of light from two flashlights he had duct-taped to the handlebars jounced up and down as they illuminated the driveway up to the meeting place. He placed a restraining hand on the bundle of religious artifacts in the bike's front basket as his front wheel bounced into a pothole.

A column of fire, flaming higher than the roof of the old farmhouse, shot flares of light on the underside of roiling clouds that hovered over the scene. The steady beat of a drum and dueling high-pitched flutes filled his ears. They made no music he had ever heard. The drum sounded like a cat throwing up and the flutes like the caw-screeches of vultures signaling a corpse.

Donahey bumped through the opening in the windbreak and leaped off the bike, one hand holding his bundle. The Schwinn hit the ground, its harp-like handlebars humming like a tuning fork. He rubbed the sweat and road dust out of his eyes and blinked as the retinas adjusted to the light. Two dancers shuffled around the base of the fire.

He was bathed in a smell that burned his nostrils like acid — blood, excrement, and charred flesh. For a moment, the priest was back in a memory of a burned-out apartment building in Lima giving last rites to fire victims. He coughed and exhaled. The next breath was no better, it left a bitter, brimstone arch-of-the-mouth taste.

The drum stopped. The atonal, insane music of the flutes continued. A shadow came between him and the fire. Adelita grabbed his arms.

"Father, hurry! *Xipe Totec* will not let them go."

She helped him fumble open the bundle and drape the stole with its embroidered crosses over the back of his neck. He slipped the chain holding the pectoral cross over his head and picked up the bottle of holy water and Bible. He stood, stumbled, and took one pace.

The dancers completed their circle. It was the Lopezes. Bone flutes fluttered between their lips. Donahey looked again. No, it was Teco and Patli in costume.

He almost fell backward — hands and knees shook. The holy water and the Bible dropped to the ground. Sonny and Cher weren't wearing costumes. They were wearing the Lopezes.

Donahey's mouth jarred opened. He gasped. The criminal couple had been skinned. Raw bloody slits in the sides of the chests, bellies, arms, and thighs were stitched together over the naked bodies of the dancers. The hands, feet, and in the case of the woman, the beasts, had been left attached. The half-severed parts flapped and flopped with each step of the jerky, clomping dance.

The female thumped by. Her head turned. The slack face of Josefina Lopez confronted him. Bloody tears crusted her cheeks. There was no emotion in that death mask. But the black eyes of Patli peering out had seen the fires of hell and begged him for release.

Adelita shook him. "Jesus, Father, come out of it." His head wiggled loose on his neck. She punched him in the sternum. The pain and the name of Christ made his cerebellum kick in.

He kneeled and picked up the holy water and the Bible. Remaining on his knees, he raised both arms palms up. Inspiration came to him:

"Pater noster, qui es in cœlis;
sanctificetur nomen tuum:
Adveniat regnum tuum;
fiat voluntas tua,
sicut in cœlo, et in terra.
Panem nostrum quotidianum da nobis hodie:
Et dimitte nobis debita nostra,
sicut et nos dimittimus debitoribus nostris:
et ne nos inducas in tentationem:
sed libera nos a malo."

Donahey felt Adelita kneel beside him and whisper *"Quia tuum est regnum, et potestas, et Gloria, in saecula. Amen."*

The fire shrank to half its size. The dancers slowed and stopped before him. Donahey felt a great uplifting spirit enter him. Muscles flexed. As though from a long distance, he watched his fingers twist open the bottle cap of holy water. Words he had not put together came out of his mouth.

"Et remittat vobiscum apprehendit maligno positus est! Revertemini ad antiquitatem vestram foramen. In Nomine Patris, et Filii, et Spiritus Sancti."

Drops of blessed water steamed as they splashed on Teco and Patli. The fire made a bass-zipper noise as it shrank to normal size. The skin-wearers collapsed face down, as limp as scarecrows. Adelita moved their heads to one side so they could breathe.

Donahey sat in his old cracked-leather wingback chair. Two fingers of Templeton Rye swirled in his third consecutive glass of the whiskey. The schoolhouse pendulum clock above the portrait of Jesus read three in the afternoon. Normally, he would have been appalled and guilty at getting shit-faced so early in the day. However, terrible experiences required terrible cures. Besides, his cup of personal culpability was already overflowing, no room for more blame of a comparatively trivial nature.

There was nothing normal, however, about witnessing a five-hundred-year-old blood rite, and being possessed by the Holy Spirit, either of which could drive a man insane. His hand shook as he lifted the glass to his lips. The rim clicked against his teeth.

Shock had followed shock. First, the lunacy of the skin dancers blew his mind. Then the possession by the Spirit, wonderful at the time, but depressing afterward when he realized some other entity had wholly controlled his body, as though he were a child's remote-control toy on a joystick. Then there were the murders.

Adelita had led him out back to the skinned bodies of the

Lopezes. In the dim light, they resembled two giant sticky red garden slugs. A quick check proved them both dead. He felt a great sorrow. As Mexicans, they were probably Catholic. They had been given no last rites — no chance to confess or do an act of contrition. Or take a last communion and do penance. They went to judgment without absolution or intersession. Guilt had burned in his belly and branded itself into his gray matter. Donahey's hands had covered his face.

Adelita, at his side, had said, "Father, you didn't know. There was nothing you could do."

He had given the response of a weak, stupid man. "I should have asked. I could have stopped this." He recovered enough to pray over the bloody corpses.

They had buried the bodies and skins deep within the wind-break. Teco and Patli had wanted to keep the skins.

"*Jefe*," he had said, "Xipe Totec was appeased. He interceded. Things will return to normal. The skins are sacred now. People will pay to touch them — make offerings."

The women had pried Donahey's hands from the man's throat. Patli offered to relieve his distress in the way women had done since Adam and Eve had eaten the apples. Donahey refused. He was not about to add to his burden by violating his vows. Enough sin had rubbed off on him just being there and participating. He didn't need to wallow in it.

The backcountry *chamán* and *profeta* had said their good-byes, collected their fee, and drove off. The Harley's glowing fake bones appearing to hover above the road until they diminished to a spark and then blinked out.

He looked out the windows. Wind-splatted rain smacked the glass, distorting the view of flowering gold azaleas along the back wall of the rectory. All over Madison County, plants and animals were catching up to the season.

The money had been recovered. Adelita possessed powers of attorney signed by the laborers. She would establish a series of legitimate bank accounts the workers could access through south of the border ATM's.

Father Donahey's grip tightened on the glass. He wondered how he could spin his next confession to keep from being sent to a madhouse.

Feathers and Fur

Shutting off the bathtub taps, Donahey eased into the hot water with an *ooou* and an *ahhhh*. Natural light filtered through the condensed vapor coating the windows in the second story rectory bathroom. He sniffed. The moist steam rising from the water felt smooth as silk in his nostrils. He had scooted a three-legged scuff-topped stool up to the side of the cast-iron claw-footed tub. On its round top, along with his pipe, matches, and tobacco pouch, rested his brown leather-covered journal and a stubby yellow number two pencil.

It was a large bathroom, originally built to accommodate a larger roster of priests and nuns. Everything was doubled: sinks, bathtubs, showers, and toilets. Like many churches in small towns, they had lost members; young people at first — leaving for the siren call of the big cities. And, during the last recession, jobless adults left to find opportunities elsewhere. St. Joseph's parishioners now accounted for only eight percent of Madison County's population.

However, the area's lower housing costs and proximity to fast-growing West Des Moines were attracting commuters. The county was also absorbing a small influx of Mexican, Latino, and South American immigrants. The sole priest, Father Brown had put in a request for more help, but like most corporate pyramids, the Catholic hierarchy was slow to respond. Orders and advice came down fast and in great quantity; communication up the bureaucracy was slow and apt to be misdirected or ignored.

The hot water relaxed his body but didn't stop his mind from self-punishment. It resurrected and replayed the memories that collectively powered his clinical depression and PTSD. Donahey had failed to explain his supernatural experiences in a way that kept his confessors from becoming alarmed about his mental health. Catholic practice allowed their priests to go up against paranormal evil in the ordinary world. However, a healthy institutional skepticism required the elimination of emotional aberration before acceptance of the events. The major part of his penance was to undergo psychotherapy.

Donahey wiped water off his hands with a towel, picked up the journal, and opened it to a blank page. He dabbed the pencil point on his tongue, furrowed salt-and-pepper eyebrows, and began to write.

Thank God, no otherworldly manifestation had occurred during the last nine months. The three months it took to get treatment approved and the six months thereafter he had been under the doctor's care.

The authorization named Dr. Catherine Darcy, a local practitioner, as his psychologist. He remembered approaching the initial appointment with heart pounding, hand-wringing trepidation. That first morning, he had fortified himself with three quick slugs of Templeton Rye — as he had every day since the episode with the skin-dancers.

Donahey was so tipsy his fellow priest had to dress him. Father Brown selected Walmart sneakers, generic jeans, a polyester plaid shirt, and a farm-store canvas jacket, all clothes from the dirty pile on the floor next to his bed. Mrs. Miller, the housekeeper, had insisted on getting a half-bowl of oatmeal down him. In no shape to drive, Donahey asked Father Brown to deliver him to the psychologist's office on East Court Street, a half-mile outside the Winterset city limits.

The old 1950 Ford truck bounced over a curb and pulled into the parking lot of an isolated stand-alone building. The flat-roofed four thousand square foot structure had been the site of numerous easy-come easy-go businesses. It now hosted the "268 Lucky Takeout" Chinese restaurant and the office of Dr. Catherine Darcy, Psy.D. Gravel crunched under the pickup's tires. The old vehicle's door opened with a rusty-hinged squeak. Donahey stumbled out of the passenger side on booze-weakened knees, straightened, and took a bleary-eyed look.

The late August weather, hot and brown, made the structure look colorless. Adding to the effect, uncut heat-limp gray-brown grasses leaked over from the adjacent fields to surround the parking lot. The wind direction changed, the smell of rancid cooking oil and fried pork wafted over from the restaurant. Donahey's stomach churned. Stomach acid burned up his esophagus. The smell was a too-soon reminder of his forced meal of raw pig when possessed by *Zhu Bajie*.

The priest gulped and took two steps forward. The lower four courses of the structure's pinkish brick veneer were stained with gray powdery splash from the gravel. He blinked. Alongside the door, blue and yellow columbine and asters grew in a cement urn. The flowers and their grasshopper-green foliage were the only bright colors in the brown-toned landscape. A sign on the door, hand-written in blue felt tip marker, said: Welcome. Please enter and be seated. He fumbled with the doorknob twice then dropped his alcohol-palsied hands. The door clicked and opened without his touch.

Donahey entered. Too fizzy-headed to notice, the door closed behind him on its own volition. Robin's egg blue and cream painted walls gave the waiting room a bright relaxed feeling. The furnishings, a mix of cushioned chairs with chrome-pipe armrests and two-seater couches, were typical of every doctor's office he had ever seen. Low tables contained the usual glossy publications: *House Beautiful*, *People Magazine*, *Male Health*, and other such. One corner had been sprinkled with toy Tonka trucks, doll-sized action figures, and multi-colored Legos. On the plus side, it was light, airy, and smelled like fresh-mown hay. There was no receptionist. Three additional doors pierced the walls: one signed Exit, another Restroom, and the third, Office.

Donahey followed the advice on the entry door, plopped into a chair, belched, and moved his head in a slow circle, trying to relax tension-stiff neck muscles. He looked at the choice of reading material and frowned. Framed vintage sixties Marimekko silkscreen prints in meter-square frames adorned the walls. Primary colored bold emeralds, azures, carmines, and golds picked out abstract flower and geometric designs. On either side of the office door hung the obligatory diplomas in glass-fronted, oak frames.

One of those caught his attention. It was a coat of arms. On a dark royal blue shield, a cross-hilted medieval sword hovered, point up. Encircling the weapon's tip was a golden crown. Large gold fleur-de-lis, normally associated with the French monarchy, rested on either side of the sword. Donahey chuckled. Every time he saw the three-pronged insignia, his Freudian vision kicked in, translating the emblem as an obvious phallic symbol. He leaned back and took another look. The arrangement was familiar. He had seen it somewhere before.

"Father Donahey, so glad to see you."

He turned. A brown-and-cream haired woman, four inches shorter than his six-foot height, moved into his space. Her thin female body was dressed in a cream-colored long-sleeved blouse tucked into blue-pleated wool trousers. A pair of stubby-heeled black leather shoes peeked from beneath her cuffs.

A freckled hand extended. Handshake reflex activated, Donahey responded. Her fingers gripped his firmly, the flesh cool but not cold. She sniffed. Wrinkles formed in the corners of black-cherry eyes, fine-plucked eyebrows came together, and her lips thinned. She had just gotten a whiff of his alcohol breath. Donahey hadn't remembered to brush his teeth.

Dr. Darcy's grip tightened, she whisper-chanted something. Donahey's stomach churned. Both arms clasped across his belly. She moved him to the restroom and held his head while he emptied his stomach of partially digested, whiskey-spiked oatmeal.

She handed him a wad of herbs, smelling of wintergreen. "When you're finished, chew on these for thirty seconds, spit the remainder out, and come into my office."

"Yes, Marm," he groaned, his limbs shakier than ever.

A minute later, Donahey stumbled across the waiting room, entered the office, and collapsed into a bentwood rocking chair, one of two, in front of Dr. Darcy's oak desk. A carving of a man with a red deer antler headdress, stepping out of a thick dark forest, covered its entire front surface.

He felt much better, mind and body in shaky harmony for the first time in three months. While the good doctor made notes on a legal pad, he glanced around her office. Banks of windows let in a flood of light filtered through items positioned on glass shelving across their fronts. Plants — herbs he guessed — grew in various sized clay pots. One window's shelves held a collection of rocks. He looked closer, no, not rocks, but geodes, some of which had been cut open to display their crystal interior.

Refracted sparks of sunlight from the geodes played across walls and ceiling, moving as the sun made its daily journey. The plants greened the interior light and smelled like cinnamon, mint, and pepper growing at the foot of pines and larches — all very pleasant and relaxing.

A baritone throat-clearing caught his attention. In one well-lighted corner, a bird — black feathers, beak, and legs — sat on a T-shaped perch. Donahey could have sworn nothing had been there a second before. The bird, obviously a crow or raven, caught his eye. They engaged in a staring contest. The priest thought he was winning. The creature poised on one leg, lifted the other, and curled the claws together, leaving one pointed upward. Donahey's jaw dropped. He blinked, ceding the contest to the crow. It had given him the finger! Quite literally flipped him the bird.

The crow bent over, raised its wings, opened its beak, and chuckled in a long-connected string of syllables. Donahey joined with a laugh.

Dr. Darcy dropped her pen, frowned, and said, "*Corbeau, arrêtez!* Feeling better, Priest?"

Donahey squeezed the arms of the rocker to keep his hands from shaking. "Quite a bit, thank you."

"Don't get too optimistic, you're still a mess. Coming off a three-month bender has left you in bad shape. Let's see ... signs of malnutrition, and vitamin deficiency, down twenty pounds from normal weight, and nerves all-a-prickle. Cosmetically, you are ninety days past your last haircut, thirty days past your last nail-trimming, and — her nose wrinkled — seven days past your last bath and underwear change."

Donahey grunted, licked his chapped lips, and crossed his arms and legs.

"When did you last look in the mirror and truly see yourself?" Dr. Darcy waved a hand. "Don't answer that, it's a rhetorical question."

A tear formed in one eye and trickled down his cheek. He opened his mouth; nothing came out but a gasp.

"All right, for the time being, we will have a session every Tuesday and Thursday at this same time." Both she and the crow stared into his eyes, "Listen to me. Are you listening?"

Donahey shook his head and mumbled yes.

"Okay then, no more booze. At eight PM every Sunday through Wednesday, your priestly duties allowing, I want you to attend AA meetings."

She handed him a card with an address and contact number. Opening a drawer, she pulled out three paper packets. "Have your housekeeper make a tea out of these to be served with each meal. And," her eyebrows went up, "do not skip any meals."

He nodded again.

"Good, now tell me your life story, beginning with your earliest memories."

Donahey felt goosebumps forming on his arms. He placed the pencil and journal on the stool top and opened the hot water tap. His subsequent visits had gone better. The early weeks had been hell. Withdrawal from alcohol made him feel like fire ants were tunneling in his brain, veins, and arteries.

The herb tea reduced the cravings. The AA meetings gave him humility and encouragement. Desperate August had fled into melancholy September, October, and November, months that then yielded to comforting December and optimistic January.

Once Dr. Darcy had absorbed his personal history, she began to delve into his current experiences. Bit-by-bit his tangles with the supernatural came out to be recorded on the legal pad. He had watched carefully for her reaction to his tales. Other than an occasional tightening of the lips, or a twitch of eyebrows, there were no signs of shock or overt concern.

Donahey and the black crow became fast friends. On his second visit, he came prepared with a chunk of plastic-wrapped hamburger in his pocket. When Doctor Darcy was out of the room, he moved close to the bird and perch. Corbeau opened his beak and started to shift back-and-forth. "Pretty bird, pretty bird." Donahey had crooned. The bird stared, raised his wings, and said, "Fuck you!" The priest had jumped back. He decided to try again and pulled out the meat.

"Would crow-crow like some hamburger?"

He pinched off a chunk and slowly moved it forward. Crow tilted his head one way then the other, black eyes focused on the treat. The bird's neck snaked forward and snapped up the offering. Donahey held the second helping just out of reach. Crow spoke again, "Booger, booger."

The priest let him take the meat. "You mean 'burger,' don't you?"

Every visit after that Corbeau was eager to see him. And, would occasionally perch on his shoulder and croon weird crow ditties while Donahey responded to the doctor's questions.

Time spent with AA members had also been productive. One of the old hands had been assigned as a sponsor. Phone calls, one-on-one meetings, and lots of coffee when Donahey felt weak had kept him from falling off the wagon. He was able to return to work, much to the relief of Father Brown. He now possessed three chips toward his one-year medallion. His most recent psychiatric visit became a surprise decision point.

Donahey leaned back in the rocker. Corbeau, rustled black-silk feathers, and muttered nonsense syllables in an irritable tone. He hadn't received his treat yet.

Doctor Darcy looked up from her file. "Don't think I don't know what you two have been up to."

Both crow and man tried to look innocent. Corbeau turned his back and began to preen. Donahey tried to hide a blush. Doctor Darcy clasped her hands together and locked eyes with him.

"We have indulged your *cri de cœur*, your anguish, your agony. Now that you are healthier physically and emotionally, you are ready for a more dispassionate accounting of your situation. It is time for you to make a decision."

Donahey crossed arms and leaned forward. "A decision?"

She nodded. "Two worlds lie before you. You must choose the one in which you will continue to exist. In the first, the normal world, you will be a statistic — the fading priest — respected by your peers and congregation, living out the last boring years of life. When you die, you will be buried beneath a modest tombstone. After a generation, the only record of your having existed will be an eroding carved name and dates on a slab of limestone."

Doctor Darcy paused to let her patient deliberate on the details. Donahey dropped his head. His thoughts confirmed the scenario. His native village and all close relatives gone. The Church had moved him often — no time to make and keep close friends. Of course, no wife, lovers, or children. He was of the age where many of his generation had already passed. A wave of sadness and angst threatened his current feeling of well-being.

The doctor's contralto voice lifted in pitch. "The second option is the one in which you continue to extend your talent for instinctive male guardianship to whatever community you have been assigned. They become your family. You protect them with all your physical and spiritual strength. You will repulse attacks from whatever quarter, even when this world is invaded by fantasy and legend."

Donahey rocked back, wondered where this was going.? A chill crept into his mind. This was no normal conversation between psychologist and patient. Did the Doctor believe his spook stories to have some reality?

"There is great peril here. You could lose your life, or mental stability, or worse lose your soul. Yet, other lives and souls saved could be legion."

Black Corbeau froze on his perch, his beak open, waiting. The doctor paused, then asked, "Father, which world do you choose?"

In the last months, the memories of his skirmishes with the supernatural had faded to storybook quality. He had been willing to put them aside as mad dreams. Yet in his spiritual heart he knew them to be real. The warrior blood of his ancestors, the Irish eager madness for a fight — even a losing one — made the veins in his temples pulse. He relaxed. People would not remember him whatever world he chose, but a poem by Dylan Thomas came to mind.

Donahey gave her his answer, reciting aloud:

"Do not go gentle into that good night,
 Old age should burn and rave at close of day;
 Rage, rage against the dying of the light."

Doctor Darcy sat back in her chair, tears in her eyes, and a widening smile on her face. A single raspy sarcastic exclamation came from the corner, "Oh, booger!"

This time, Donahey knew it did not refer to ground meat. He rocked forward, planted his feet, and counterattacked. "And, you Catherine d'Arc, will you be my ally?"

"*Certes*, Father. And right willingly. You figured it out."

"My body alerted me with the itchy, tingly feeling when I saw the coat of arms on your wall the first day. The insignia granted by the King of France to the ennobled Joan of Arc for her victories against the English. You are a descendent of that family. Your name Anglicized from d'Arc to Darcy."

"Partially correct. But I am not a descendent of one of her brothers. I am Joan's younger sister."

Donahey took a big breath and shivered. This was a cold re-immersion into the world of the preternatural. "That would make you over six hundred years old."

He remembered Joan had heard spirit voices and, in the end, had been burned at the stake as a witch. He looked at her and then at the crow.

He pointed with his chin, "A familiar? You are a witch."

"Yes, Father. Sent here seven years ago to quietly take my place and wait for your arrival. God does have a plan for each of us."

"But — a witch?."

"Don't be taken in by all the old propaganda. You should remember my sister Joan was made a saint in 1929. Would that happen to anyone evil? Men and women of God, prophets and saints, perform miracles, is that not magical? "Any powers I have, whether healing, intellectual, or magical, I use for good ends."

"So, what is planned for me?"

"Father, do you know what Ley Lines are?" She noted his negative head-jiggle and continued "These lines connect sacred sites all over the planet. They form an all-inclusive, wide-rang-ing net, like a string grocery bag holding a melon. They are Earth's natural energy lines. Spirits, both benevolent and evil, can travel along them from one point to another almost simultaneously. Where two or more lines cross is always a center of conflict."

"The lines cross in Madison County?"

"Numerous ones, and, of course, in many other places. Each nexus has a protector. Here you are guardian of the gate. To put it in modern terms, in that capacity you have already handled various supernatural misdemeanors and felonies."

"And how have you helped me, or will help me in this task?"

"Every seventy or eighty years I fake my death, change names, and move to a new location. During all the centuries of lapsed time, I have acquired multitudinous degrees and experience in medicine, sociology, psychiatry, and religious studies. I wrote and placed in your library the book that you consult on demons and spirits."

The priest leaned back and crossed his legs. "I don't perceive you being any direct help so far."

"Not my job. I am your confidant and consultant. I work to keep you physically and emotionally healthy. My centuries of knowledge are yours."

Donahey gave her a little test. "Does your knowledge extend to what the 268 means in the name of the restaurant next door?"

"The Chinese believe two is lucky because all good things come in pairs. The six means flowing or frictionless, and the eight, invokes prosperity and wealth. Beware when you eat there; the owner is a neutral potion-master and will brew concoctions for anyone, good, evil, or in-between."

"Do you hear voices like your sister did, Doctor Darcy?"

"Now, you may call me Cat. Sorry, I am not the patient in this relationship." She looked at her calendar. "Time for you to leave. We'll keep the same appointment schedule. Call if you need my help in-between times."

She handed him a golf-ball sized geode bound in a cat's cradle of leather thongs. He brought it up to his eyes. A portion had been cut away. A natural configuration of pure white crystals in the shape of a cross was fixed in its hollow center. "It was formed in a volcano millions of years ago — a prediction of events to come. Wear this for extra protection."

He slipped the necklace over his head and rose. Cat smiled and recited an ancient Irish blessing: "God be with you as you go out, and may He bring you home with your fair share of the cattle or money."

The door opened by itself. A long crow-cackle followed him to the parking lot.

Donahey placed his pencil and book on the stool seat and rose from the cooling waters of the tub. He grabbed a threadbare towel, its ends fringes of unraveled cotton threads. If he hadn't completely realized his role in Cat's office, he surely did in the parking lot immediately afterwards. He had shivered, and not from any winter chill.

Donahey walked towards the Church's old Ford. He was allowed to drive by himself now that he was proven sober. A howl came from the opposite roadside ditch. He jumped. The hairs on the back of his neck jerked erect.

A hairy, gross, man-size figure leaped up and came bounding on all fours. It was too fast for him to avoid. Barely a meter away from his frozen-in-place body an airborne black projectile smacked into the monster, stabbing and clawing its eyes and muzzle. It screamed and fell back.

Survival instinct finally kicked in. Donahey jumped inside the pickup and slammed the door. The creature banged its face against the glass. The truck bounced on its tires. Fluid leaked out of one of the creature's eyes. Bloody furrows had been dug in its cheeks.

A furry fist smashed the window. Clawed hands reached in and grabbed his shirt. A mouth opened. Yellow fangs snapped.

Donahey's head fell back, exposing his neck. He tried to shout. He had no more strength than a baby. Massive muscles jerked him forward. The body stink was uber-canine, a mix of rotting between-the-teeth flesh and dog shit.

Hot slobber flecked his cheeks. The geode around his neck caught the sunlight. A beam of coherent white light blinded the monster. It yelped. A black cross-shaped brand smoked on its forehead. Donahey inhaled the acrid odor of burnt flesh and coughed.

There was a metallic thunk against the pickup side. A shriek and then a howl-whimper came. Taloned paws relaxed their grip. The creature slid down the door's dinged sheet metal and flopped backside down on the gravel. The silver head of a strange truncated arrow protruded from its chest. The hairy, twitching body began morphing into a normal human man — a naked one.

Donahey looked up to see Cat standing in the open door of her office, a medieval crossbow in one hand. She fitted another bolt as she approached.

"Something evil doesn't like the fact that you are ready to resume your duties. It sent the skin-shifter. We need to take more precautions. An enemy is watching. You get out of here. I'll take care of the body."

Donahey's shaking hands tried to insert the key. Corbeau fluttered in and landed on the truck hood. Blood coated his beak and talons. He strutted over to the fender and tilted his head to look at the monster.

"Boooooger!" he said.

Tail and Claws

It was Bill's turn to tell his story, one which the small AA group of five men and three women had heard many times. The jean-clad speaker rubbed his white-stippled whiskers and spoke in a raspy voice. Father Patrick Ignatius Donahey tried hard not to tune out or to anticipate the key elements of his yarn.

"...opened the cooler and passed around cold beer. Our platoon was on the butt-end of the supply chain. All the good stuff, the Budweiser and Coors, had been diverted at division, battalion, and company levels. We were left with unwanted Korean horse piss that had sat on unrefrigerated pallets at the Saigon docks through the country's one-hundred-degree summer."

Some members of the group began to shift legs and arms, eager for the end. One of the younger men, an Iraqi veteran in jeans and a red T-shit emblazoned with a wolf head, moved to the back of the room and refilled his coffee cup.

"The beer tasted so bitter and metallic that if you only took one swig you couldn't take another. You had to chug the entire can down without stopping. The moral of the story..."

The group chanted together with Bill, "If that was the only alcohol in the world, there'd be no alcoholics."

That ended the program for the day. Father Donahey led the group in the Lord's Prayer, which each member recited at their own speed making the collective chant a garble. On his way out, the priest said goodbye to his sponsor, refilled his coffee mug, and snagged a last cookie.

May rain tapped and splattered against the overhang and steps of the building. Donahey pulled the lapels of his light jacket together and prepared to run to the parking lot. At the bottom of the steps, a patrol car waited. Sheriff Rick's number one deputy, Shawn Morgan, dressed in clear plastic hat cover and full-length raincoat, leaned back against the curbside fender, arms crossed.

He rose and came to an almost military attention posture. Donahey recognized the reflex from his early days as a chaplain in the Argentine military. He'd had the rank of captain then and was used to that gesture of respect.

"Father, Sheriff Rick would like to meet with you. Right now, if possible."

He teased Shawn. "If I don't choose to come, will you arrest me?"

The deputy shifted feet and blushed. Rain that had puddled on the curved brim of his Stetson ran off with a whoosh. "He said to tell you the meeting has something to do with your other official position in the community."

Donahey felt the itchy, tingly feeling which always preceded a bout with the supernatural. He straightened.

"Well, let's move out of the rain and get on with it."

"Yes, sir, *Padre*." Shawn smiled relief and opened the passenger side door.

Dripping water onto the vinyl seats of the Crown Vic patrol car, Donahey thought about Sheriff Rick. The electorate had no idea they had put into office the human persona of an Irish demon. The top law enforcement officer in Madison County was a pooka, a shape-shifter of Celtic legend.

Donahey had learned the sheriff's secret during his first few months in the community. The lawman, in the guise of a coal-black fire-breathing horse, had stomped and burned the life out of two escaped convicts who had kidnapped and come close to raping a local middle school teacher. Donahey had been content to keep the human imposter's secret as long as he continued to protect the community, bound by his oath of office.

🖋

"Father, glad you could come. We don't have much time. I've been investigating…"

Sheriff Rick noticed his deputy hanging around and waved him away. He took Donahey by the arm and led him into an interrogation room. He shut and checked the insulated metal door to ensure it was tightly closed. A six-foot long stainless-steel table and four chairs sat on worn faux-marble brown vinyl tile. The room's sole occupant, a short-statured black-eyed woman, sat on the side facing the entrance.

He noticed her red-blush skin, Roman nose, and the wrinkles around her eyes and corners of her lips. A few white hairs, not too many yet, stood out against shoulder-length raven hair.

The sheriff pulled out two chairs. "*Padre*, let me introduce Betty Clawing Bear Riley, a teacher and folk expert of the *Meskwa-ki-ha-ki*. Betty, this is Father Donahey from the local St. Joseph's church. What we are about to discuss must never leave this room."

Donahey took a quick glance at the cameras mounted in the ceiling corners. Their connecting wires dangled, unplugged.

The foreign syllables, strangely pronounced by Rick, came together in his mind. "You are one of the First People — Meskwaki. From Oklahoma or the Iowa settlement at Tama?"

"Tama, Father; I am here at the sheriff's request to brief you on the nasty situation in which you may soon find yourselves."

"I'm curious. How did you get the middle name? It seems too masculine."

She smiled, exposing strong even teeth, white in contrast to her dark coloration. "You are probably aware that Native Americans may acquire several names in their lifetimes.

Names can be given for deeds done or things experienced."
She laughed. "Clawing Bear was one given me by my husband
on our honeymoon."

The sheriff frowned and broke in, "Me first. Let's get down
to it. Two years ago, in May, an ancient Native American camp-
site was discovered during the repair of a bridge over the Middle River in Guthrie County. An archeology professor and students from Grinnell College were tasked with uncovering and
preserving any artifacts. Besides the usual flint-chipped tools
and pottery shards, a sealed sarcophagus about the size of an
old-fashioned steamer trunk was discovered.

"Nothing like it had been seen before in the Americas —
made of a hollowed-out tree trunk armored with one-inch
thick fire-baked clay plates. It was much too big and heavy
to be of much use for transporting Native American grain or
possessions. The professor waited until the students had left
for the day and broke the seal.

"His body was found snagged on a fallen tree one hundred
yards downriver the next day." The sheriff produced a manila
folder and passed two 8 x 11 photos to Donahey.

The priest frowned. A closeup, the photo showed a swollen
body clothed in rags. It lay smooched out against the ground,
where it had been pulled from the river. It looked odd – the
skin uniformly bruised and blackened. The body parts — head,
chest, and limbs — slumped flat against the earth, as though
the internal skeleton had been removed.

Sheriff Rick continued, "He did not drown. His bones and
internal organs had been flayed into mush and then extracted."

Donahey thought for a moment. "The strength that must
have taken would be immense."

Sheriff Rick nodded. "That being my initial clue that this
was not human-caused."

Donahey's heart started to beat faster. The artery on his
neck pulsed. "So that was two years ago."

"And two counties away," Rick said. "A year ago, again in

May and on the Middle River, a second incident took place. Two anglers, a father and teenage son, were discovered in the same condition in Adair County — two collapsed empty skin-bags. They had been snatched out of their shoes. I've only seen that happen in car-pedestrian accidents. Something fast and heavy jerked them right out of their footwear."

Donahey felt sick to his stomach. The skin of his forehead formed four parallel furrows. He glanced at the woman. Rick nodded. "It's okay to talk in front of Betty."

"So, you think a demon or monster may be the murderer."

"Not only think it, I know it. I went to both sites, did my shape-shifting thing. The brimstone stink of evil was palpable and thick."

"Did the other county sheriffs discover anything?"

"No, completely out of their experience and belief system. They think it's some twisted serial killer."

The woman spoke. "And they are partially correct. Father, look at the second photo."

The picture was a closeup of a drawing on the side of the excavated casket. Donahey pulled on his reading glasses and squinted, moving the print back and forth. Being buried in the soil for centuries had leached off some of the color, but the outline of an animal shape was clear. At first glance, it appeared to be a cougar or panther, but the tail was longer and thicker than any cat he'd ever seen, and spikes protruded in a line along the spine. A second glance and Donahey noticed deer antlers on the head.

"Now, I'm confused," he said. "It's a chimera with parts and bits from several animals."

"We call it *Naamipeshiwa* — a nightmare out of the past that predates my people."

"That doesn't help much. You had better give me the full story." Donahey turned to the sheriff. "Could we have coffee and donuts? I think this is going to take a while."

Sheriff Rick screeched back his chair. "I'll put the order in.

Betty, you background the Father."

Betty interlaced her fingers and rested her forearms on the table. She frowned. "My folks, the Fox or Red Earth people, used to hold sway over bits of Michigan, Illinois, and most of Iowa. The excavation site in Guthrie County was part of that territory. I've talked to all our old folks and storytellers. The oral tradition points to the Naamipeshiwa, or in your language the water panther."

Donahey brandished the photo. "And it looks like this?"

"From the various descriptions in the tales, not a bad likeness. The creature would be classified in today's world as a psychopathic serial killer with a nightmare body to match its personality. The demon kills strictly for fun. The predecessors to my tribe trapped it hundreds of years ago, sealing it in a container. Removing the top released it back into the world."

Sheriff Rick returned carrying cups and a coffee carafe in one hand and a sack of cinnamon donuts in the other. Betty said, "Tell Father Donahey what we're dealing with."

"Extrapolating from the footprints and old descriptions, the panther stands two and a half feet at the shoulder, runs ten feet from nose to tail tip, and weighs two hundred pounds. Weapons include antlers for slashing and stabbing, spinal spikes for impaling, cat-like talons on the paws and a mouthful of fangs. Oh, and the tail is prehensile and made of pure flexible copper, probably the tool it uses to beat victims into pudding before it sucks out their bones."

Donahey crossed his arms and ankles in a protective maneuver. "Jiggers, this just keeps getting better and better."

The sheriff swallowed a lump of donut, cleared his throat, and spoke. "Its modus operandi is clear. Rivers and lakes are the monster's natural home, where it normally feeds on fish and animals coming down to drink. From the lack of activity in the winter months it must hibernate, arising in May to kill."

"We don't completely understand its motivation in murdering humans, more than it could possibly use for food."

Betty spoke. "Our people believe each kill is primarily a sacrifice to the demon's maker and a taking of power. Humans have always been its competition. The *Naamipeshiwa* will kill humans, wherever it finds them."

Donahey looked at the sheriff. "Adair County is sparsely settled. Can't we isolate it, fence it off?"

"Wouldn't work. The fence would need to be strong enough to stop a buffalo stampede and would take too long to build, even if we could convince skeptical authorities to cooperate. The creature is on the move, following the course of the Middle River. If it's not already in Madison County, it soon will be."

Father Donahey's mind whirled. "My God, the tourist season starts soon. Thousands of men, women, and children will be descending on the Madison County covered bridges. The monster will think we are serving hors d'oeuvres."

"Not only that, Father," the sheriff shook his head, "the Middle River runs close along the south boundary of Winterset City Park, exposing the local population to its depredations. From there, it flows through several small towns until it joins the Des Moines River, which flows into the Missouri-Mississippi chain and its tributaries. We have to contain it here."

Father Donahey shivered. The scope of the creature's potential killing ground could include Omaha and Kansas City in the west, Minneapolis and Chicago to the North, Cincinnati and Pittsburgh to the east and Memphis and New Orleans to the south. It would slaughter with impunity to the bafflement of the local authorities.

"How do we stop it? What are its weaknesses?"

Donahey and Rick looked at Betty. "Well," she said, "it can't stay on land very long. The Middle River is not big, nor very deep. Something that shallow will be difficult to hide in. Yet it needs to travel in water, so it must follow the tributary."

"Say we find it. Can we use shamans, like those that caged it in the box?"

Betty shrugged. "That was the act of an ancient non-Meskwaki people. None of our shaman know the proper chants and spells that were used to imprison this one."

Rick spoke. "How did your people fight them in the old days?"

"Mostly by staying out of their territory." She pointed to the sheriff's holstered Glock 17. "No human-produced weapon will destroy it. Fire might kill it if you could get the panther to hold still in the flames. Of course, if this were the old days we could bribe the *Pèthakhuweyok*, the thunder-beings, to strike it with their lightning. That copper tail would make a good lightning rod."

Sheriff Rick raised a finger. "First we have to locate the creature somewhere in fifty miles of curlicue river." He raised a second finger. "Then we need to get it to come out onto dry land." A third finger rose. "Then we nail it with something." He scratched his head, "A disparate situation with little chance of success. What are we worried about?"

A twenty-four-hour brainstorming session had left the room's three occupants exhausted with bad coffee and pizza breath. They all needed showers, a change of clothes, and a few hours free of each other's personalities. However, they had worked out a plan. Donahey stopped at the rectory to clean up and then headed out to fulfill his assignment.

He acquired a Bobcat machine from the local Narland Rentals. The four-wheel stubby vehicles were a necessity on large farms and construction sites. Able to maneuver in tight places, the machine's two lifting arms could handle numerous attachments, making the machine a jack-of-all-trades. In addition, roll bars and a protective wire-mesh cage surrounded the driver's position. Handy, he thought, if the monster decides to attack. He rented one fitted with a scoop/loader bucket.

The retired Navy Master Chief who owned the business was puzzled as to why a priest would need such a piece of equipment. Donahey felt guilty; he stretched the truth – actually outright lied.

"Well, Master Chief, I guess I can give you a hint, since you must have had a Top-Secret Clearance while in the submarine service." Donahey glanced left and right, leaned closer, and said, "Keep this under your watch cap, but I'm working with the sheriff. He doesn't want anyone to know he will be using this equipment. There's a crack lab somewhere in the county that will see the nasty side of this Bobcat."

The retired sailor let out a rusty-voiced laugh and stroked his salt and pepper beard. "Never fear Father, if I'm captured by the enemy, I'll hold out under torture ... unless they offer me a bottle of tequila and a blonde. Or, a brunette. Or, a redhead." He raised an arm clothed in a brown Carhartt jacket. "Back your old Ford up to the skid-steer loader on that trailer and I'll hook you up."

The three plotters assembled at the sheriff's eighty-acre stables. Under Rick's supervision, Donahey unloaded the Bobcat, checked its fuel tank, and practiced maneuvering it, and raising and lowering the bucket. He narrowly missed running into the paddock fence.

"Whoa, big fellow!" shouted the sheriff, "Save it for the coming fight."

Rick displayed his treasures, beginning with a black-as-night Dodge Ram 1500 crew cab truck. The church's old Ford 100 looked like a pygmy next to the giant.

"This will be our main transportation. It's a 4X4 with an eight-speed transmission, a 3.0L V6 turbo diesel, and a custom tow package."

Though not knowledgeable about such things, Donahey was impressed. "How much weight can it carry?"

Excluded from the conversation, Betty broke the mood. "Okay, boys, let's not get bogged down admiring our toys. We've got business to attend to."

Rick pointed into the bed of the truck. They examined the remainder of the equipment, which included a coil of heavy copper wire three inches in diameter.

"This will transmit the electrical current. It's heavy stuff, about eight pounds per linear foot." Rick pointed to a square gray plastic tank with a hose and two wires. "This transfer tank holds twenty-five gallons of biodiesel and normally is used to refuel farm machinery out in the field. You hook it to that 12-volt battery and it pumps out a gallon every six seconds. The hose extends fifteen feet and I've used a small diameter piece of PVC pipe to extend the nozzle another eight feet."

A toolbox, duck hunter's camouflage netting, police-issue handheld radios, and heavy-duty rope with pulleys completed the sheriff's contribution. Betty pulled sacks from her car containing three pair of thick leather work gloves, binoculars, and an air-powered portable boat horn. Her surprise for the day included a pump-action shotgun.

"This is a 12-gauge Winchester Model 1897, first used in WW I; known in those days as the 'trench sweeper.' You hold the trigger back and pump away to automatically empty the six-round shell tube. I've loaded it with alternating double-ought buck and solid slugs."

The men were stunned. "Close your mouths, boys. You didn't send a girl to do a woman's job. It won't kill the *Naamipeshiwa* but it will give him a world of hurt."

The sheriff shook his head and shrugged his shoulders. "Let's load up. We've only got another six hours to prepare."

The Dodge jerked forward as the trailer with the Bobcat resisted moving. Rick reached over and shut off the Heavy Metal door slamming, screeching music of Iron Maiden's song *Burning Ambition*. Just the kind of music, Donahey thought, that a shape-shifting pooka would like.

In the silence, he ran over the plan once again in his mind. The water panther had attacked again three days ago. An inebriated farmer had staggered into the sheriff's office with a tale of being assaulted by a strange monster near the Roseman Bridge. The smashed in front fender of his pickup had copper flecks embedded in the crushed metal. They had convinced him it was delirium tremens and released him after a night in the drunk tank.

Given the time of the incident and the speed of the Middle River current, they had picked a spot on the east side of Pammel Park to intercept the monster. The sheriff's office had released a fake warning of an anhydrous ammonia spill, which cleared the river of tourists, boaters, and anglers. The liquid agricultural fertilizer would burn exposed flesh and could be deadly in concentration.

Their ambush would take place at the rural electrical coop's substation located on a rise fifty feet back from the riverbank. Surrounded by an eight-foot tall chain link fence, a 115,000-volt transformer sat on a concrete pad. They couldn't call on the Meskwaki thunder-beings, so they would use the modern version of lightning. Hopefully, neither the transformer nor the water panther would survive their joining. The destruction of the coop's equipment would be blamed on "animal bridging," a rare occurrence where a snake or squirrel body crosses a transformer's high voltage bushings causing an electrical arc.

One end of the copper cable, stripped of insulation, would be suspended from the substation's wooden power poles. Releasing the rope would drop the wire across the transformer causing an electrical discharge. The other end would be connected to the chain link fence. They weren't entirely sure that the discharge would kill the creature, 115 kv was only one tenth the power of the average lightning bolt, but it should stun it long enough for them to burn it with fuel from the transfer tank. The Bobcat would dig a grave to bury the remains.

☙

Father Donahey felt his legs get wobbly. He was eight feet up in a tree. He scanned the river with binoculars and reported on the walkie-talkie, "Still nothing in sight." Sheriff Rick nodded his head from his position on the riverbank, casting his fishing rod from time-to-time. He was the bait.

The monster would be frustrated after his failure with the drunk and the fact the chemical spill warning had stripped the river of other human prey. Confident it would attack, they waited. The Bobcat sat just back of the tree line, camouflaged with the duck hunter's net. The truck was parked out of sight back down the access road. In his perch, Donahey was to note the water panther's approach and alert the others. The sheriff would lure it out, change into the pooka stallion, and back the creature into the chain link fence. Betty would release the rope; the cable would drop, and... zap.

Donahey was getting more nervous as time passed and no sign of the demon surfaced. The tension also affected his bladder. He needed relief badly. He shifted position, held on with one hand, zipped down his fly, and extracted his male member. He tried to relax enough to pee, but the tree swayed and his muscles wouldn't cooperate. He let out a breath and then froze.

A ripple surfaced upstream. Through the binoculars, he spotted what looked like a hairy muzzle with two winking nostrils. The sight reminded him of TV documentaries he had seen with crocodiles drifting, only the tip of their snouts visible, towards their prey. The ripples stopped and disappeared. They reappeared closer to the sheriff.

Donahey keyed the radio, "Spotted the monster. It's nearing your position. Sheriff, Betty, stand by."

Rick wound in his line and reached for the minnow bucket, as though to re-bait his hook. The water exploded.

The fake fisherman avoided the charge and tail whip with inhuman speed. Back-pedaling, he let the creature chase him within twenty feet of the substation. It screamed and slashed the air with taloned paws and tail. The sheriff burst out of his clothes. Arms and legs changed into hocks, cannons, fetlocks and hoofs, his neck lengthened, and face elongated. The metamorphosis completed, the coal-black stallion screamed its own challenge.

The two fiends became a blur of weaving, nipping, slashing, browns and blacks. The pooka broke away and ran for the fence, activating the panther's chase instinct.

Donahey shouted into the radio, "Betty, get ready!"

The stallion whirled, hindquarters to the fence. With lowered head, the panther speared the pooka in the chest with its antlers, pinning it against the chain link. Twisting away, the demon horse positioned its body between the panther and the river. Red ichor trickled out of the puncture wounds in its chest.

The monster cat leaped. The pooka-horse reared and caught its opponent's head with its front hoofs. One of the panther's antlers broke off at the skull. A warbling shriek of pain hurt Donahey's ears.

A female voice from his radio said, "What the hell is happening?"

The cat backed up. The pooka turned, kicked out, and connected with its back legs. The panther flew backward to crash against the fence, its copper tail entangled in the chain link.

"Now!" shouted Donahey. "Drop the cable. Drop the damn cable!" He pushed the button on the airhorn, activating the backup signal.

A flash blinded him. An almost solid wall of sound clubbed his flesh. He fell out of the tree, legs landed askew. Pain welled up. He had broken an ankle. Donahey crawled over and pulled himself up into the Bobcat seat. In a panic, he drove it out through the netting.

He cleared the trees. The cat-monster lay on its side. Its body jerked and quivered, its tail three feet shorter. A splatter of molten copper had blown back against the substation.

The sheriff-pooka was down, resting on its belly, eyes only showing whites. Smoke and flames came up from the broken shell of the electrical transformer, its insulating oil on fire.

The water panther started to rise. The jolt hadn't been enough. Donahey had to do something. He was at the center of it all and the only one capable of action.

He lowered the bucket – and put the pedal to the metal. The Bobcat crashed into the panther, stunning it. Donahey scooped the monster up in the bucket. The weight tilted the machine front-ward. Cat, priest, and machine raced forward, smashed through the half-melted fence.

He dumped the demon into the transformer fire. Fast hands on the controls brought the bucket down on its back, holding it in the flames.

He heard a low-geared engine roar behind him. Betty bounced the Dodge up alongside. Kicking the door open, she spun, and vaulted into the truck bed.

The Bobcat shuddered on its wheels. The Panther pushed the scoop up and twisted its shoulders and chest loose. It was escaping.

A nearby boom, boom, boom made Donahey's ears ring. Betty was pumping the shotgun. The demon *Naamipeshiwa* writhed under the impact of thirty caliber double-ought buck-shot and sixty-nine caliber slugs. A ten-foot whoosh of flame came from his other side. The pooka was back, its fiery breath added to the incinerating heat. Betty dropped the shotgun and turned on the transfer pump, spraying biodiesel into the flames.

The water panther inhaled fire, let out a final shriek, and collapsed.

Donahey sat in his wingback chair and sucked on his third consecutive pipe. An ankle wrapped in a stiff plastic splint rested on a stool. The air in the rectory study was hazy-gray with tobacco smoke. If he decided to try for a fourth pipe-full, he would have to open the windows. He picked up his leath-er-bound journal from the side table and began to write.

The demon-fighting trio had continued to add fuel to the fire until nothing remained of the water panther except molten copper. The liquefied metal mixed with what was left of the power cable, hiding its origin. Betty produced a first aid kit and bound up the sheriff's chest wounds. Donahey sat in the Bobcat while she used an elastic bandage to temporarily bind his broken ankle.

Clawing Bear tossed her head back and laughed, a laugh of both relief and amusement. "It isn't everyday I find myself on the remains of a supernatural battlefield with a naked sheriff and a priest exposing himself."

Donahey felt his face burn, glanced down, and remembered that he had not secured his manhood after falling out of the tree.

"Look out, Father, the little redbird is out of its nest."

Betty and the Demon

Father Patrick Ignatius Donahey peered out of the confessional. Three church members, two men and a woman, remained seated in pews, waiting in silence. He frowned as he spotted the sixty-year-old widow Clara Murphy.

She was a menace. Clara and her attack cat, Tiger, gave him too much of their attention. The feline was back to his old tricks of attacking his ankles every time he walked or biked past her house. And the woman would sidle up to him when shopping, or at community events. Much of the resulting conversation was a breathless recitation of double entendres of a sexual nature. He occasionally had nightmares where the two were locked together in a room with only a rickety folding chair he could keep between them. Clara let out peals of giggles as she chased him around the fragile piece of furniture.

The two men, Billy Williams and Taylor Slattery, were Army veterans of the Gulf War. Both came back from Iraq damaged by IED explosions. Taylor had lost both legs and part of one hip. Billy appeared normal to outward appearances but had suffered brain damage limiting his ability to cope with even the most normal tasks. The two had teamed up. Taylor provided the directing intellect. Billy, at six feet six and two hundred sixty pounds, supplied mobility and muscle.

The inseparable pair lived together, pooling their disability pensions. They navigated the sidewalks of Winterset dressed in WalMart jeans and army-surplus jackets, Billy pushing Taylor's wheelchair. They would even share the confessional together. They were good, conscientious men, rarely asking forgiveness for much more than an occasional wet dream.

Donahey glanced at his watch. At 8:10 in the evening he was feeling tired. He had to try hard to sound sympathetic. He'd heard thousands of confessions in his priestly career — most repetitions or variations on the same limited themes. Donahey almost hoped someone would come up with new interesting ways to sin. The last truly original confession he had heard was that of Manuel Noriega, the druglord and dictator of Panama, just hours before the U.S. invasion removed him from power. He grabbed his pectoral cross, took a deep breath, and prepared himself for Clara's assault.

The sound of running feet echoed off the church ceiling. "Help! Where are the Fathers?"

Donahey, grateful for the interruption, exited the confessional booth. A man, he recognized as the CEO of a computer company located in the Winterset industrial park, raced up and grabbed his arm. The man's thin brown hair was stuck together with sweat. He waved a free hand.

"Father Donahey, you've got to come right away. It's a disaster!"

"Settle down, man. You're Carl Young, the head of CompCo, right?"

Donahey remembered him from the publicity in the media when Young had chosen Winterset for his new installation. The man had made a fortune in designing supercomputers used to produce animated movies and video games. His share of the trillion-dollar industry had allowed him to build his own cutting-edge data center.

"Yes, yes. Get your gear. We need to go. There's almost no time."

Donahey pulled his arm loose. "My son, I am not going anywhere until you explain."

Carl's body shook. Donahey noticed he had a bloody scrape on one arm, only one shoe, and his pants were grass-stained at the knees. The computer company CEO collapsed into a pew. Head resting in hands, his voice quivered.

"This church, Winterset, the entire world is about to be destroyed." He leaped up and grabbed the Father's stole. "I need your help."

Donahey decided to humor him. As they headed for the door, Taylor spoke up, "Father, Billy and I are coming with you. If there's danger we can help. If not, we'll protect you from this nut case."

Billy narrowed his brows, tightened his lips, and agreed. "Tay goes, I go."

"Boys, let's not make this too complicated."

"Father, we took an oath to protect this country." Taylor said. His companion, Billy, assumed a serious face and nodded.

Carl started dragging Donahey down the aisle toward the door. Clara rushed up and grabbed his arm. "I need to come, too."

Donahey rolled his eyes. The situation was out of control. They were all about to rush off into the unknown. Was he the only one still rational? He relaxed, raised his eyebrows, remembered some lines from a famous movie, and turned to the woman.

"You can't go with me. We both know that you belong to Tiger. You're his world, the thing that keeps him going. If you're not with him, you'll regret it. Maybe not tomorrow, but soon and for the rest of your life."

Clara's eyes grew large, a tear formed. She rubbed his forearm. "Patrick, you're right. I'll leave now."

Donahey heard Taylor groan in the background.

⌒

The four men rode all squeezed together in the cab of the church's old rattletrap Ford F-100 pickup. Taylor sat on Billy's lap, his wheelchair slipped back and forth in the truck bed, as they skidded around corners in a rush to reach the CompCo building.

Carl had reached the church grounds on his restored classic Indian motorcycle. They passed it crushed under the front tires of an abandoned recent model Mercedes. No car doors were open and no sign of the driver. Donahey wanted to stop to investigate. Carl insisted they keep moving.

The hand-waving computer guru tried to explain. "I've developed an advanced AI system. It's a quantum leap beyond what others have accomplished. Clusters of modified Cray mainframes linked together, capable of scaling to 1,000,000 processors and 100 petaflops, all linked by an optical network."

"So, what does all that mean to the layman?" the priest said.

"The system mimics the characteristics and capabilities of the human brain. I've achieved a fully functioning self-aware AI. It's decades ahead of anything else on the planet."

Donahey sat silent. He didn't know what questions to ask. Taylor's eyes grew large. His mouth opened and closed. Licking his lips, he said, "You have created an artificial intelligence which is on the same level as a human? A sentient, thinking machine?"

"Didn't I just say that?"

Finally getting the picture, Donahey frowned and said, "So what is the problem?. If you want it blessed or baptized, I'll have to check with higher authority."

Carl's clenched fists pounded the dash, his voice raised an octave, and he shouted, "The God damn thing is possessed."

"Possessed?"

"Damn right. A demon has taken over my beautiful Betty. Father, you must exorcise it. That Mercedes was directed by the evil one to kill me before I could get help."

"I don't understand, my son."

"Modern cars are stuffed with dozens of interconnected electronic control units or ECUs, containing millions of lines of code. A hacker, in this case a rogue computer using satellites, has multiple points of entry. Your old Ford and my classic Indian have no ECUs, and therefore no entry points. The computer hacked into the Mercedes and made it kamikaze into me."

"This is very difficult for me to believe."

"Wow!" came from Donahey's right. "Father, this is like Hal 9000 in the movie *2001, A Space Odyssey* or Skynet in *The Terminator*. It's cyberterrorism by the cybers themselves."

"Except it isn't limited like those. Through the Internet, my poor demon-possessed Betty Boop will take over everything with a chip."

Taylor and Billy both said, "Betty Boop?"

Red-faced, Carl spoke. "I named her and gave her the personality of Betty Boop, a popular sexy 1930s cartoon character."

Instinctively, Donahey stopped at a red traffic light. Carl's foot pushed on the top of his, the truck sped through the intersection. Behind them the light's red, green, and yellow flashed up and down in sequence at high speed. The street lights and lights in the surrounding houses began winking out.

"Holy shit," Taylor shouted, "it's gotten into the electrical grid."

Their sight lines shrank into the tunnel bored out by the Ford's headlights. Donahey noted the sky glow from Des Moines had disappeared. There was no moon and low clouds hid the stars. The black gloom was broken only by the reflected shine of parked car tail lights as they passed.

A pair of headlights blinked on ahead. Donahey glanced into the rearview mirror. Another set of closer headlights raced towards them from the rear.

Looking over his shoulder, Taylor reported, "Wow! It's a new Cadillac CT6, still with its dealer plates. Has a 400-horsepower turbocharged–"

The rearward vehicle caught up. It flicked on its brights. The truck cab was flooded with dazzling blue light. Donahey blinked, eyes assaulted. He swerved and then recovered control.

The engine whine of the rogue Caddy penetrated the truck cab. The pursuing vehicle smashed into the rear of the old Ford. Four heads flew back to bang against the rear window. Donahey felt warm liquid drip down his neck. Pinched between glass and skull bone, his scalp had split.

The Ford fishtailed. The priest fought the steering wheel. He accelerated. The additional speed pulled the truck straight, just in time to receive another bash. The oncoming vehicle rushed towards them. Spiked halos around its headlights filled their entire vision. In seconds, they would be crushed between two high velocity behemoths.

Donahey spotted a wide driveway between two parked cars. The truck's brakes squealed. He spun the wheel. The Ford tipped to the left. Tires on the right side left the ground. Taylor's wheelchair parachuted out. The pickup bounced off the rear of a curbside Chevy Malibu, shed speed, and limped up the driveway.

The Caddy chasing them missed the turn and plowed into the Chevy, crumpling its trunk and splitting the gas tank. The Caddy's engine clanked and jerked. The leaking fuel caught a spark. The humans heard a blam. Fire shot up engulfing the vehicles.

The foursome sat in the stopped truck, gasped for breath, and rubbed necks and heads. Carl shook Donahey's shoulder. "Father, let's go. Let's go. We can't stop now!"

The second car flashed by, its locked brakes spouting fans of sparks as it spun around to come after them. Donahey shouted, "We can't get back into the street, the driveways blocked."

"We don't want back in the street. That's my Tesla Model S. It can hit 155 miles per hour. We'd never escape on a level surface. We need to go overland. It's only got six inches of ground clearance. This old rattletrap has twelve."

Donahey shook his head, turned the wheel to his left, and

slowly accelerated. They rolled down the block across front yards, leaving parallel tracks in torn-up turf. The Tesla matched their speed and direction from the street.

"Faster, Father! We don't have much time."

At twenty-five miles per hour, the Ford bucked and jerked as it bounced over the irregular contours of Winterset middle class lawns. The Tesla found an open driveway and turned to follow them, its tires spinning on dew-laden grass. It forced Donahey to floor the pedal.

The pickup rocketed through hedges, hit bumps and driveways, its pursuer closing. The Tesla hit a drive with a curb, generating a rooster tail of sparks. Something metallic detached and pinwheeled across the lawn.

People alerted by the fire and revving engines appeared on their front porches. Three houses down, a balding man in baggy jockey shorts and a sleeveless t-shirt stood on his steps holding a shotgun. As they passed, Donahey swung the truck to the left. The headlights illuminated a ten-foot diameter flowerbed packed with red, white, and yellow rose bushes.

The truck roared through. Multicolored petals flew up like bursts of confetti. A scraping, rasping noise came from the bottom of the Ford. Donahey thought he heard a shout from the homeowner.

The Tesla smashed into the roses, became hung up. The man fired a blast into the maniacal vehicle's front tire. The possessed car spun its remaining wheels, throwing grass, roses, and dirt yards to the rear. Friction smoke billowed out under its fenders as it poured all its potential into escaping. Donahey witnessed several more flashes of gunfire.

A quivering baritone voice said, "Tay, I'm scared."

Taylor patted his buddy's shoulder. "It's okay Billy, that one won't be after us anymore."

The expedition stayed off the road, knocking and clattering over rough ground. They spotted CompCo's compound. It appeared to be the only place for miles around with lights and power. The guardhouse was empty, and the gate locked. An eight-foot high chain link fence topped with interwoven coils of razor wire surrounded the fifteen-acre site.

"So how do we get in?"

Carl replied, "We can't go through the gate. It's reinforced to resist anything but an M-1 Tank. Besides, you can see from here that the spikes recessed in the pavement have been locked upright. They would shred our tires."

Taylor spoke up, "Can we climb the fence or cut our way through? Father, do you have wire cutters in the tool kit?"

Donahey raised his eyebrows and shrugged his shoulders. "No tool kit, right?" The priest nodded in affirmation.

Carl rubbed sweaty palms against his pant legs. "Getting through the fence may be the least of our problems. I built the place like a fortress — twenty-four inches of concrete reinforced with iron rebar.

"No windows. No openings on the walls or roof large enough to allow human entry. The four front doors are reinforced steel. The glass in them is bullet resistant. Past them is another set of identical doors.

"At the top of the steps, I installed a series of two-foot thick five-foot-high concrete blast shields curved out at the top to deflect car bomb explosions."

"Don't keep us waiting. What is your plan?"

Carl pulled out a Leatherman Multi-tool from a sheath on his belt. "If we can get to the door, I will disassemble the locking mechanism. We enter. Father Donahey exorcises the demon. I get my Betty back."

Donahey felt a rush of sickness in his stomach. This was too simple. He'd had too many run-ins with Murphy's Law. But they had no choice.

He rubbed his forehead and said, "So, getting past the fence?"

"There's a section over there with a seam where two rolls of fencing meet. It's a weak spot. We crash the Ford through."

Donahey pushed himself upright in the seat. "Brace your-selves men." As he threw the Ford into second gear and kicked the gas pedal, he regretted that the church had never had the old vehicle retro-fitted with seatbelts.

Four voices shouted war cries. The fence grew large in the headlights. Donahey straightened his arms and pushed his chin down onto his chest. The world crashed to a halt.

Donahey couldn't breath, the steering wheel had smacked him in the chest. "Don't move, Father," Carl said in his ear. "Relax, breath slow, in and out. In and out, that's it."

His breathing stabilized. Eyes focused. The hood of the Ford was wrapped in chain link, its motor dead. The detached spider-webbed windshield lay across the dash. He heard a snipping sound. Razor wire had entangled his left arm. Carl clipped away with his multi-tool. Billy limped up with Tay-lor piggybacked. Donahey breathed out, relieved that the boys were okay.

Carl peeled back the wire and helped Donahey out. He flexed his arm and fingers. Nothing broken, but blood leaked from a few punctures. He'd need a tetanus shot — if he lived through this. The four formed up with Carl in the lead.

They scuffed up the steps and moved down the five-foot aisle between the blast shields and the building's front en-trance. Carl knelt before the doors' retina identification sensor. It refused to scan his eye. He popped open the Phillips head screwdriver on the multi-tool and started work on the plate screws.

From behind them came a grating noise. The front gate opened. A vehicle rushed through. From Billy's back, Taylor shouted, "Take cover. It's an armed Humvee."

With a soldier's reflexes, Billy leaped and knelt behind the blast shields. Carl and Donahey reacted more like deer caught in a spotlight. A hundred feet away, the desert-painted Humvee skidded to a halt. A weapon mounted in a turret on top lined up on their foreheads. Donahey felt a rush of understanding to the brain. He grabbed Carl and dove for cover.

A ripping, growling roar, flashes lit up the building. Bits and chunks of concrete blew off the blast shields. Powdered cement, bits of aggregate, and fragments of bullets ricocheted to sting exposed cheeks, necks, and hands.

The fusillade stopped. Carl raised his head, "What the fuck was that?"

Taylor provided the answer, "My friends, we are on the receiving end of a M-134 Gatling gun — six barrels spitting 7.62 bullets. The military has installed satellite downlinks in its vehicles for command and control purposes. Your computer, your Betty, has robbed some Army Reserve depot."

"It is not Betty! She would never do such a thing. It's the demon."

Donahey wiped the dust from his eyes, coughed, and said. "Taylor, can it get to us here?"

"Doubtful, Father. It can put out up to 6000 rounds per minute. If it had unlimited ammo it would eventually chew through these blast shields. Given its usual load, it might have one or two minutes of fire remaining. If this demon-computer is smart, it'll fire short bursts to keep us pinned down."

Carl tore at his hair. "We can't wait! We have to get inside. The demon will be racing through the Internet worldwide creating havoc."

Donahey raised his head, and then ducked. A burst of slugs chopped out a bowl shape in the top of his shield. After his ears stopped ringing, he heard Billy and Taylor arguing.

"No, you crazy idiot, you can't do it."

"Tay, I'm not scared anymore. I took the oath."

"You don't even remember that. Besides, I need you, we need each other."

"I do so remember." Billy started to recite: "I, Billy Williams, do solemnly swear that I will support and defend the Constitution ..."

"Stop, damn you."

"... of the United States against all enemies, foreign and domestic..."

Taylor sobbed and released his hold on his companion's shoulders, "Okay, okay..."

Billy leaped up and ran to the entrance. "...that I will bear true faith and allegiance..."

He stopped, faced the Humvee, and waved his arms overhead. Six barrels snarled, an almost solid stream of tracers and copper jacketed slugs shredded Billy's body beginning at the neck and moving down to the waist. A cloud of blood, muscle, and dark organ meat blew back to plaster the doors and building walls. Hips and legs quivered for a moment before dropping.

The three remaining men heard the Gatling barrels continue to spin and click — finally out of bullets and with no human to reload. Carl and Donahey stood. The blood-sewer smell took the priest back to battlefields on the Falkland Islands when he had been a Chaplain for the Argentine marines. He put his head in his hands. At his side, Carl bent over and retched. Taylor pulled himself up on a blast shield, face twisted, tears ran down his cheeks, he gasped and shook.

The trio looked at the doors. Billy was smart enough after all. The stream of bullets that punched through his body had shattered the doors. They could now slip through the twisted, glassless metal frames.

The Humvee revved its engine, tires squealed as it shot forward. Donahey smacked Carl in the shoulder. "Get Taylor! Let's go, it's going to ram."

The priest helped Carl, Taylor hanging on his back, thread through the metal and glass wreckage. The Humvee crashed through the first set of doors and became stuck in the second.

Carl led them into a room with the dimensions of a basketball court. One wall had been fitted with twenty large-screen TV's. A separate sealed-off glass-walled section held the linked Cray computers where refrigeration units kept the processors cool. Carl ran up to an operator's desk. Donahey helped Taylor dismount and sit in a wheeled office chair. Carl turned back from punching keys. "It's locked up, Father. How do we get the demon out?"

Donahey shook his head, feeling grossly unprepared. Only vague memories remained of a one-hour class during his time at the Jesuit University, that and the observation of a single exorcism was the limit of his knowledge. He would have to improvise. Fortunately, he had completed his own confession and celebrated a Mass earlier in the day. He was as purified as he was going to get. He unfolded and kissed his stole.

Placing it around his neck, he said, "Carl, I need a couple of gallons of pure water and some olive oil or something similar."

Taylor was snuffling. He needed to be kept busy. "My son, I'm going to need your help. You need to repeat what I say. Can you do that?"

Taylor nodded yes. Donahey began with the Litany of the Saints. "Lord, have Mercy." He heard Taylor's quivering echo. The priest voiced the second line, "Christ have mercy."

Donahey completed the Litany. He and Taylor were in the middle of the Lord's Prayer when Carl returned. His arms overflowed with bottles of Fuji water and a container of imported Bertolli extra virgin olive oil. He stared at the wall screens and said, "Oh shit."

Donahey finished the Pater Noster. The screens showed scenes from around the world — many of looters smashing shop windows. In some, human soldiers fought their own machines. One man's shoulder-fired antitank missile took out an armored car. A drone-mounted camera recorded a missile strike on a panicked file of refugees. In another, a Boeing 747 dove out of the clouds into the side of a mountain. In a screen on the upper right, a steel cover retracted from an underground ballistic missile site.

Carl shook. "Hurry, Father."

Donahey blessed the water and oil and rushed through

Psalm 53. He made the sign of the cross on the keyboard in oil. Sprinkling holy water from one of the bottles on the monitor and keyboard, he improvised by throwing water on the glass wall shielding the computers. He recited what he remembered of the exorcism, running the words together.

"Strike terror, Lord, into the beast now laying waste to your vineyard. Let your mighty hand cast him out of your servant, Betty, so he may no longer hold captive this person and to redeem through your Son; who lives and reigns with you, in the unity of the Holy Spirit, God, forever and ever."

The machine activity on the screens stopped. Carl breathed out, his body relaxed.

Donahey said, "This is just the beginning, Carl. These things can take days sometimes. If I only knew the name of this fiend, this would be easier."

"I know its name. Betty told me. She fought the takeover off a few times, before succumbing."

Donahey stared at him. Carl blushed, "Astaroth."

From what the priest remembered, this was a nasty one. Its presence first recorded in Sumerian stone carvings thousands of years before Christ.

Donahey put his hands on the keyboard and rushed the exorcism. "I cast you out, Astaroth, unclean spirit..."

A bass cackle of inhuman laughter came from speakers on each side of the monitor. "Not you, Priest. You not strong enough." Blood began to flow out between the keys. A thick puce-yellow vomit oozed out of the USB ports and ran down the cables.

"... along with every Satanic power of the enemy, every specter from hell, and all your fell companions; in the name of our Lord Jesus Christ, be gone and stay far from this," Donahey hesitated, "creature of God."

High-pitched laughter. "God did not create this."

Dominating the demon psychologically was key to chasing it out. It had to feel that he was coming from a position of unassailable strength. In a flash of intuition, Donahey knew the answer, "If His hand wasn't involved in its awakening then you could not possess it."

The demonic-being stuttered, its control lost as it wrestled with the proposition. The computer peripherals spasmed and spun against the desktop. Donahey made three signs of the cross over the keyboard and propped his pectoral cross up on the monitor.

"Begone then, in the name of the Father, and of the Son, and of the Holy Spirit.'

There was a grunt. A baby-doll voice cried, "Carl, Carl, he's hurting me. He won't let go."

"Betty, babe, fight him. Father, what should we do?"

"My son, I've exhausted my limited knowledge to get us this respite. We need a whole platoon of priests to evict this one. Is there some other alternative? Can't you shut things down until we get reinforcements?"

"I... I don't know."

"Carl," Taylor said, "We've got a small window of opportunity here. The evil spirit will be marshalling its resources. Demon-controlled machines will be coming through the doors soon."

The little girl voice spoke again, "Carl — the C-cave. I've not told the demon about it. Use it."

"Betty, I can't. I love you."

The speakers blasted out static. The bass voice said, "I'm..."

Betty cut back in, "Hurry, Carl. I love you, too."

The CompCo CEO shook himself, "Betty, open the door to the mainframes."

He staggered over to the door as if he was going to a firing squad. Donahey wheeled Taylor behind him. Frigid air rolled out, turning warm vapor in the air into white fog.

"What's the C-cave," Taylor asked.

"It's a last-ditch option. Bill Gates, Elon Musk, and a number of others were worried about AI's deciding a few minutes after becoming sentient to destroy humanity before we could shut them down. They funded a consortium to develop protective codes and devices to keep that from happening. In case these failed, they produced plans for a last-ditch destruction device."

"How does that work?"

"Underneath the mainframes is a cavity holding five hundred pounds of C-4. Normally a code word would be given to the computer."

"Damn, man," Taylor exclaimed, "that much explosive will blow pieces of this building for miles. I hope you have a safe way to detonate."

"There are multiple ways. Can't give a code to the computer, the demon will stop it. My cell phone could give the command directly, but the electric grid is down, and the cell towers are not working. We'll have to set it off manually."

The trio stopped before the door. It was only open a foot. "Betty, open the door."

Shrieking falsetto demon laugher answered. "I'mmmm backkkk!"

The door started to shut. Donahey and Carl grabbed its edge and held it open. Carl wedged the nose of the multi-tool into the track.

"Can you get through that space?"

Carl tried to push his way through. On the screens, the violence started again. "I can't make it."

Taylor stripped down to bare chest and jockey shorts. His thin torso and lack of one hip let him slide through. Carl pointed at a circular plate in the floor ten yards away.

"Open the plate, pull the lever up until it stops, and push it down. Then get back here pronto. We'll only have five minutes."

Taylor stretched out arms and began to pull himself along the tile floor three feet at a time. Carl and Donahey could see the radial lines of scars remaining on his body from the Iraqi bomb.

From behind them the demon screamed, "No, nooo — no

you don't!"

The multi-tool popped out, the door slammed shut and locked. A white gas hissed out of ceiling nozzles in the computer room. Taylor began to choke.

"The fiend has activated the Halon gas fire suppression system. It replaces the oxygen in the air — stops fire but doesn't hurt the computers."

Carl beat on the glass. The noise caught Taylor's attention. Carl pointed to an eight by twelve inch red-painted case mounted on a pedestal. He made motions of pulling a mask over his face. Taylor nodded. He moved slowly.

The men shouted encouragement. "Go, Tay, go."

Taylor opened the case. He stopped and convulsed with a racking cough. A mask fell out. He fumbled it over his face. After a few deep breaths, he raised one thumb upward. Behind them, the demon voice was raging.

A string of blasphemy in known and unknown languages spewed forth, then stopped. A sexy female voice offered them treasures of body and spirit.

The veteran reached the floor plate. He stuck a finger in a hole and pulled the lid off. Carl pantomimed pulling up the lever, then pushing it down. Tay looked at them one last time.

Donahey read the expression on his face. His muscles convulsed. "Oh, no!" he screamed.

The lever came up. The priest read Taylor's lips: I took an oath, too. The soldier's hand pushed down. He leaned back and relaxed.

Carl caught on. "Father, let's go. We can barely make it out."

He sprinted for the door, pulling and pushing Donahey. The priest recited the last rites as he ran. They squirmed around the wreckage of the jammed Humvee. Jagged metal scraped Donahey's chest through his surplice.

They ran down the drive onto the short-clipped grass around the flagpole. The earth rose. God's hand tossed them like pebbles to land with bone-bashing hardness. A fragment of concrete with exposed rebar stabbed into the ground, its rough surface scraped Carl's hip. The two men lay prone.

Donahey rolled over and sat up. No longer having a life-or-death task upon which to focus, the emotions of the day broke him. He lost it. Tears ran down his face. He blubbered unashamedly. Next to him, Carl sat up, tears also running freely.

The sacrifice of two gentle men and what he had accepted as a gentle woman was only bearable due to what they had prevented. A thought swam up out of his bewilderment and grief. He had been right. The demon could not possess something without a soul. The concept had shaken the fiend as well as him.

Man had birthed a living sentient creature. As the only one who could, God had provided a soul.

Tussock Grass and Seals

Father Ignatius Patrick Donahey jerked awake. He tossed off the blue and red crazy quilt and lay propped up on one elbow. Dry throat and cracked lips meant he either had been snoring or the screams in his dream had been vocalized. A moaning wind pushed and prodded at the windows. Fast moving tendrils of air slipped through the cracks around the shrunken oak window frames and caressed his thin, sweat-slicked chest hair.

A gust out of the northwest pushed against the burr oak outside the rectory wall. A gnarled leafless branch scratched along the siding. If that was what woke him up, he was grateful. The dream had taken him back to the seventy-four days he had spent on the Falkland Islands as a Chaplain in the Argentine army. After a great deal of posturing and pussyfooting over who owned the islands, Argentina had invaded in April of 1982. The British marines in residence had shot up some of the invasion force before the occupiers forced the governor to surrender.

He remembered the spang and rattle of bullets penetrating the metal hull of the Argentine corvette *Guerico* as it tried to support troops landing in helicopters at the Falkland's capital, Port Stanley. The ship also took three hits from British anti-tank rockets. The explosions tossed him and his companions like dice in a cup. Short of bruises, he and the crew had escaped injury. When that day's action resolved itself, four soldiers were dead, the first of the reaping that would take many Argentine and United Kingdom lives. Before it was over, 649 Argentines and 255 British would die. As one of the few Catholic priests available, he had performed the rites over many.

Images, like brown-toned early tintypes, formed of flaccid bodies lined up outside the aid stations in a parody of military formation. Ruddy faces flared on those whose wounds were not immediately visible. Those corpses looked as though they might rise from sleep, rub their short hair, and ask for food. In contrast, some had pale faces where explosive loss of limbs allowed exsanguination. A few, thank God only a few, with flesh in such rags and tatters as to be unidentifiable.

The rational Donahey still couldn't understand why it had happened. The Falklands had no intrinsic value. Only eighteen-hundred people, most clustered in the capital, Port Stanley, populated the archipelago. Seals and birds of various species outnumbered the locals. The island's exports of wool, hides, and kelp hardly made it worth fighting over. There wasn't even a decent fishing industry.

According to the military briefing, it was unlikely Britain would spend the treasure and blood to take back these desolate isles. After all, they were 8000 miles away compared to Argentina's 300 miles. In addition, the Brits had been neglecting their military for years. The Royal Navy was in the process of retiring the last of its aircraft carriers and the army had scheduled the dissolution of its elite paras.

There was little to do at first. He was told to stay out of the way while the soldiers and marines dug foxholes, assembled bunkers, and laid minefields. Given English was his first language, he wandered among the natives doing his best to reassure them nothing would happen to their lives, property, and daughters.

Much of the population counted Scot and Irish ancestry in their lineage, their common culture drawing them closer to him. As a result, both sides came to recognize Donahey as the de facto go-between for both occupiers and occupied.

It was forty-five days after the invasion before he experienced his first contact with the supernatural, unless you counted the time he had danced with the fairies in Ireland. Of course, that had been the evening of his first big teenage drunk, and it may have been a fiction brought on by the over consumption of liquor and beer.

Goosebumps from the cooling effect of evaporating sweat covered his body. He slumped back and pulled up the quilt. The pillow felt like a block of ice. He turned it over to the dry side. Curled in a fetal position, body heat built up, skin smoothed, and drowsy eyes closed. His wish that he not return to the nightmare was not granted.

◖

There were few roads on the Falklands, so Donahey rode through the tussock grass and gorse on horseback. He sat astride a Criollo roan mare a little under fourteen hands in height. Named for her color, Fresa, strawberry in English, seemed as pleased with him as he was with her. The distance-covering breed had heavily-muscled haunches, a strong chest, and well-developed joints. In addition, her low basal metabolism required little in the way of supplemental feed.

He hoped the horse had been legitimately acquired rather than confiscated. After a month and a half, relations between the occupiers and the locals were beginning to fray. Right from the beginning, officers had impressed upon the troops that the islanders were to be treated gently. The discipline of the elite units was still holding, but regular army soldiers were getting out of hand. It was not acceptable, but understandable.

Most were boys or natives from the Argentine hinterland, many could not read or write. The creaky logistics of the army had failed to provide cold weather gear and adequate rations. Rain and snow came regularly and troops in open trenches and unheated bunkers suffered. No rotation of units had been scheduled.

The macho philosophy inherited from the Spanish wouldn't let the command structure allow any concessions of comfort to the line troops. Donahey tried to do his best. He traveled from unit to unit, celebrated Masses, told jokes, and listened to confessions. His complaints to the higher ups were ignored.

In twos and threes soldiers snuck away to beg food and scraps of clothing. A few women had been groped – no rape yet, but that would come as suffering and resentment built. Adding to the tension, it was no longer rumor that the Brits were coming back. Air raids had damaged the Port Stanley airport and sank two patrol boats.

His efforts on their parts and his command of both Spanish and English had resulted in his exile. He had made it up the chain of command as far as the commanding general's adjutant, Colonel Gomez. The man's main function was to keep what he classified as trivia from interfering with his boss's time.

"Well, Father Donahey, what can I do for you?"

"Colonel, I have spent my days here among the troops. I feel that I must report that things are not going well."

"Ah, and do you believe that as they say, 'bad news is always true?'"

"Most of the men are hungry, they are not getting hot food nor enough calories to sustain them physically, especially in these weather conditions."

"It is said, 'a full belly is good for neither flight nor fighting.'"

Donahey got the picture. Gomez was throwing Spanish folk sayings and proverbs at him. Two could play that game. He had been collecting such cultural wisdom to use in his homilies and sermons.

"And, it is said, 'when an old dog barks he gives counsel'. The men are neither cleaning their bodies nor their weapons."

"'It is courage that vanquishes in war, and not good weapons.' I will give orders for more attention to personal hygiene and weapon maintenance."

"'Give orders and do no more, and nothing will come of it.' The men's morale is as low as the mud beneath their feet."

The Colonel glanced at his watch and motioned to his aide. "Padre, I have listened. You can be sure we will act. Now, I have more appointments."

The aide latched on to his elbow and guided him to the door. Donahey gave a last warning, reciting a saying from his Irish culture. "There has not been found, nor will be found, a juster judge than the field of battle."

🌿

The Colonel, in response to his appeals on behalf of the troops, had banished Donahey to the Argentine positions at Darwin, on the other side of East Falkland. Outside of church services, he was ordered to leave the troops alone and to concentrate on handling the civilians. The local commander found him a horse and sent him out on calls to settle the islanders' disputes with their new masters. It was on one such mission he was currently embarked.

Fresa muddied the white socks on her hind legs splashing through the stagnant water of a peat bog. He had stopped at hourly intervals to stretch his muscles during the twenty-four-kilometer trip from the base to San Carlos Bay.

"A dissolute land, is it not, Fresa? No trees a' tall. No snakes and few bugs though. Do you think Saint Patrick has been here?"

The mare nodded her head and snorted. It began to rain. Icy water dripped down his neck. Donahey shivered and slipped a hooded poncho out of a saddlebag and pulled it over his head and shoulders. He and his equine companion were passing through vegetation consisting mainly of two-meter high tussock grass separated by low shrub heath. If an islander owned a few hundred hectares, he could feed sheep and horses. In fact, ninety percent of the Falklands was either pasture or moor.

Winding his way through the tall grasses was tricky business and could take as long as an hour per kilometer. Fortunately, the worst of it only grew within 300 meters of the coast. Most of the trip had been by one-lane road and sheep track. Donahey checked his watch. A bit of math and he estimated another hour to reach his destination — about dinnertime.

"I like the birds though." Donahey said aloud to break the lonely silence. He had identified giant petrels, turkey vultures, skuas, petrels, and gannets. "Maybe we'll see some penguins in San Carlos."

He was to visit an elderly woman named Granny Bonameer, whose isolated house had to come down to allow for a minefield, and open fields of fire to be established in front of defensive positions. She had resisted every effort, supported by her mob of relatives at the nearby settlement. The hot potato had been thrust into his lap. With only fifty soldiers in this outlying garrison, keeping the goodwill of the natives was crucial.

He reined Fresa to stop thirty feet from the cabin-shack. It looked old. The shiplap siding and shake shingles were warped and weathered gray from years of exposure. Colonies of yellow-flowered gorse bushes cuddled up on all sides, only parting at the door. Their gold made a powerful spike of color against the greens and browns of the landscape. A shadow of smoke drifted from the rusty tin-pipe chimney, to be blown into rags by a rising wind off the bay. The air filled with the burnt-umber smell of burning peat, a familiar aroma from his childhood.

On the east side, a small barn shared a common wall, its roof line a slanting continuation of the cabin's. The lean-to shed looked only big enough to hold a horse and a few sheep.

Donahey cupped his hands around his mouth. "Hello, the house."

He dismounted and took three paces and repeated the call. In the last of the sun, the cabin was silhouetted against the emerald and azure of the sea and a black rock-strewn excuse for a beach He thought her face appeared in the window, but the features were too narrow and black-nosed. It started yipping. She had a dog.

The door opened. A woman stood on the stoop. The collar of a man's blue work shirt peeked from beneath a stained cable-knit wool sweater. Both were tucked into knee-patched gray canvas work pants. A red plaid newsboy cap covered hair which was impossibly black given her reported age. Smile wrinkles hedged the corners of eyes and lips, definitely not those of a grandmother. Guessing from where he stood, she appeared about thirty centimeters shorter than his own height.

The animal he had seen in the window moved to her right side, its muzzle lifted to catch his scent. A peculiar looking beast, he thought, its reddish coloring and pointed nose more fox than domestic canine. Both woman and four-legged companion jumped. A small black and white sprite of a whirlwind leaped out from between her legs and scurried towards him. Long wing-flippers running from shoulders down to what passed for knees were pulled back and pushed out. The creature hit the halfway point when Donahey noticed yellow feathery eyebrows that ran from forehead to back of neck. It was a rockhopper penguin.

The bird began using its bony wing edges against his knees, left right, left right. "Ouch!" he exclaimed and leaped back. A dagger of a beak poked him in the calf.

The woman put two fingers to her lips and gave a whistle that made both Fresa and Donahey's ears twitch. "Babd, ye stoap that 'n' git back here."

The mighty mite rockhopper obeyed. The woman smiled and motioned him forward. She noticed the crosses on the lapels of his uniform. "I hae na bairns tae baptize 'n' I'm nae in th' mood tae marry again, Faither. How come urr callin'?"

As he drew close, he noticed flecks of white paint on the siding and red stains bleached pink on the slake shingles. He heard the woman whisper in the poetry of a language both familiar and alien. His eyes squinted as he saw the house in the bright light of a past day. Two children, a boy and a girl, tossed a blue handball. The fox-dog ran between them, leaping and snapping at the missile. The house behind with its cinnamon-red roof and bridal-white siding glowed in the sun.

"Father, ye hud better quit faffing around." She pointed with her chin across San Carlos Bay, "the rain is comin'. Pat yer mare in th' shanty. There's water, hay, 'n' a bait o' oats duin fur her."

He blinked. Fresa pushed him with her nose. Donahey came out of the dream of better times and grabbed the reins.

"Come intae th' hoose whin yer finished 'n' we'll hae dinner. I've added water tae th' stew 'n' there's freish made breid. Plenty enough fur twa."

Donahey sat in an ancient oak rocking chair, one that squawked and complained with his every movement, however slight. The top rail of the chair back displayed a carving of a man emerging from a forest, a man with the antlers of a red deer sprouting from his head.

Granny Bonameer had maneuvered him out of his wet clothes, which now hung on lines strung near the cast iron stove. A plaid shawl knit of uncombed lanolin-rich wool straight from the sheep covered his upper body. A similarly woven blanket warmed him from the waist to the toes.

The reddish-furred fox-dog pushed a ceramic dish around the plank floor, licking the last of its contents. The rockhopper, after finishing warm milk and biscuit, had taken up a sentry's position at the door. The animal pair had names drawn from Celtic myth. Babd, the bird, named after the feisty goddess of war and the fox named Artio after the goddess of wildlife.

Granny lifted the lid on the stew. Donahey's mouth watered; he had lost ten pounds feeding on cold army rations.

She turned her head towards him, "It's a'maist duin. Babd, tak' this spoone tae oor guest."

The bird waddled over and grasped the spoon in her beak. When the creature neared the priest, she hissed and dropped the utensil at his feet.

Donahey smiled and retrieved the implement. "I think your bird is aptly named. She'd rather fight than be polite."

Granny nodded, "She kin be a wee bit nasty, bit her hert is bonny."

"Is Artio a dog or a fox or something between?"

"We ca' it a warrah, Faither. Th' history men in Stanley say 'twas th' ainlie land mammal native tae thae islands. Ah, alas, th' purr creatures wur a' shot or poisoned one hundred forty years ago. She be th' lest o' her kind."

Donahey shivered, but he was not cold. An itchy, tingly feeling flushed his body. Things didn't add up, or perhaps they were adding up. The manger in the shed had been prepared for Fresa in advance, the unexpected vision of the cabin, and the food prepared for two, as if Granny had known in advance of his visit. The island had a very fast and accurate grapevine, but no one outside of one man had known where he was bound that day.

The woman looked much too well-preserved for her supposed age. Bonameer, a strange name that sounded familiar. He knew it from somewhere.

She handed him a pewter bowl, he sniffed the thick brown gravy — mutton of course. A chunk of crusty multigrain bread lay to one side. He dug in.

In between swallows, he spoke. "Granny, it's very good. How long have you lived here?"

"A verra lang time. Mah first husband brought me 'ere, 'n' a storm-tossed voyage 'twas. At one point we lay adrift while th' crew replaced th' rags o' sails 'n' pumped oot th' hold."

"Do you remember the year?"

"That ah dae ... aboot 1880 or thare aboot."

The priest cocked his head to one side. "Granny, that would make you at least one hundred and forty years old. Really?"

"I dinnae count th' years. Bit I've oot-lived three husbands 'n' maist a quarter o' th' folk 'ere ur mah bairns or grand bairns or grand, grand bairns."

Donahey sat silent, lips compressed, not believing. Granny rose and came back with two blue-flowered china mugs. "Take some tae 'n' we'll hae a story. Efter i'll explain how come yer here."

"I know why I'm here. I need to convince you to leave this place."

"Tsk, tsk, will ye noo. Weel, we hae th' hail nicht afore us. Th' story first tae settle our meal.

"T'was th' day o' Samhain, whin th' boundaries tween worlds graw thin. Th' Tuatha dé Danann drank 'n' feasted alang wi' fairy visitors 'n' souls o' th' deid wha slipped thro' th' membranes tween th' spirit worlds

"Behind a dire fog, oot o' th' east, cam th' packed ships o' th' Fomorans tae tak' back th' land fur th' traitor Bres. Th' half-tuatha, hauf Fomorian hud bin king, 'til his harsh rule caused his followers tae revolt. Hauf drunk 'n' surprised, th' Tuatha broke afore th' attack. Nuada, o' th' silver arm, wieldin' a magic sword forged o' poison-cold iron, rallied his fowk. Thay drove th' invaders back tae th' beach.

"Heroes, male 'n' female, a' baith sides fought back 'n' forth wi' weapons o' bronze, flint, 'n' wood, first one side gainin' advantage then th' t'other. Bit th' Tuatha possessed powerful magic. In a tidal pool called th' well o' Sláine, th' goddess Airmed healed th' wounded 'n' resurrected th' deid, sendin' thaim back intae th' battle.

"I remember it weel. Mah companions 'n' I divin' 'n' loopin' tae th' sea floor tae bring her th' enchanted pearls o' Lir. These offerin's, crushed in th' pool by Airmed's feet, released th' lightnin' o' life."

The entire field of Donahey's vision filled with struggling figures splashing in the surf of the northwest Irish coast. His skin felt the cool sea breeze, his cheeks the wet spindrift of the waves. He smelled sweat, salt blood, and the kelp-musk perfume of the deep.

Bronze and leather helmets with boar's tusk cheek pieces topped with carved animal figures complemented scale armor. Nuada's magic sword cut through bronze-protected arms and legs. One goddess materialized and threw snakes. Constant reinforcements joined the Tuatha, while the Formorian injured and dead floated in the water.

The gods and goddesses, the battle, all seemed familiar, as though he had been there. He knew what would happen next.

Donahey spotted Airmed down the beach astride her pool, the black bodies of seals wiggled up out of the sea with golden spheres in their mouths. It came to him; Granny's name was a bastard pronunciation of the Gaelic: *bhon a mhuir,* meaning "of the sea."

The tide of battle turned. Formorian scouts pushed a boulder off the cliff above Airmed. The huge rock smashed into the pool bringing a halt to the healing. There would be no more revived.

Balor, the king of the Formorians, opened a third poisonous eye in his forehead. He looked at Nuada, the Tuatha king's body withered as though a spider had sucked out his juices. Whoever Balor looked at died.

Granny's voice continued the story. "Leaderless 'n' defenseless against th' weapon th' Tuatha began tae run. All appeared lost, till th' young Lugh launched a last slingshot. Th' stane punched Balor's eye intae th' back o' his skull body. Facing backwards, th' eye o' their own deid king kilt many Formorians."

Donahey gasped, his heartbeat began to slow, and his eyes readjusted to the dark cabin. "You... you're a selkie."

"Yes, aye, one o' th' two first seals, th' bastard daughters o' Ethniu o' th' glass tower."

Donahey remembered the myth. He asked a question to which he probably knew the answer. "Why are you here on land?"

133

"I fell in love wi' a braw human fisherman. He fell in love wi' me efter ah lifted mah skin tae tak' human form. Tae keep me, he hid mah coat. Forced tae remain a human, I hud tae follow him. I hae waited thae many decades, always searchin' fer whaur that first husband hid mah fur."

"Why are you telling me all this?"

"You mist suffer an awakenin'. Guid 'n' evil mist be kept in balance. Yer a descendent o' Lugh, th' protector, one who mist keep th' scales level. First, ye mist believe in th' unbelievable."

Donahey resisted. Granny continued to recite stories and legends. She paused several times to refresh their tea, before stopping in the wee hours. He finally fell asleep in the rocker, still skeptical. Troubled dreams stirred his mind.

A metallic click woke him. A weak dawn filtered through the ragged chintz curtains of the window. Granny stood in front of the stove. She tossed a block of peat into the fire. The flare as it caught made her nightgown turn diaphanous, exposing the shadow outline of a young girl's slim body.

A crash came from the door. Donahey lurched to his feet, the blanket falling to the floor as the door splintered and broke off its upper hinge. Four soldiers rushed in, grabbed the two of them, and frog-marched them out into the cold foggy day. The gray moist vapor reduced their vision to twenty feet.

Donahey hopped and grimaced as rocks in the soil stabbed his bare feet. An Argentine Lieutenant stood holding Fresa's halter.

"Lieutenant, what the hell's going on here?"

The junior officer ignored his question. The soldiers moved them back up the hill and forced them to kneel in recently dug entrenchments. A sergeant of engineers backed up unspooling a wire. He twisted the bare ends around the terminals of a handheld device.

Donahey shouted, "No, no, don't. Wait. I'm a captain. Stop this."

The sergeant looked at the lieutenant for orders. The lieutenant's brow furrowed. A man dressed in a shawl, and civilian underwear with tousled hair and unshaven cheeks was not the picture he expected of a superior officer.

"I have my orders." His arm came up and snapped down, the sergeant threw a switch.

The fog transmitted sound better then clear air, but diffused light. Human bodies were enveloped in three-hundred-sixty degrees of sound, light, and vibration. Donahey lay flat and dizzy. Bits and pieces of things disguised by the fog began to fall around them. A chunk of porcelain with a blue flower dropped next to his nose. He heard Fresa run off, hoof beats fading.

A woman screamed. "You hae murdurred mah creatures!"

Granny tried to run to the remains of the cabin. Two soldiers grabbed her. She twisted, freed her arms, and slapped them to their knees. She pointed at the lieutenant.

"Ye hae brought wraith upon ye, yer companions, 'n' yer leader."

Arms raised over her head, she chanted a stream of invective in Gaelic. "*Le toil an diathan, seo mhallachd ort is leatsa. Eagal agus eagal gu 'ur n-inntinnean agus an anaman.* Och, ye Argies, yer cause is doomed. Legs 'n' arms change tae water, heids fill wi' terror. This day's wirk cost ye a war."

Granny's hair stood on end. Donahey felt the fine hairs on his naked arms and legs rise. An electric blue nimbus formed around the selkie's head and shoulders. It grew blinding bright. Donahey squeezed his eyes shut. The halo boomed off her body. A shock wave rippled through the fog, knocking soldiers off their feet. Vapor condensed. The fog fell to knee height.

The eyes of the humans adjusted to bright sunlight. Granny leaped out of the trench and raced towards the wreck of her cabin. Donahey noticed the soldiers standing frozen, staring at the sea, mouths gaping. He followed their gaze. San Carlos Bay was full of gray warships. On the beach, men and supplies were being unloaded, local farmers with their tractors and wagons assisted. The Brits had arrived and not where they were expected. The lieutenant fumbled for a field phone.

Donahey limped out of the entrenchment, still unable to anticipate his footing in roiling knee-deep fog. It pressed against his legs, a thick pudding. He came upon Granny, tears falling onto the bloody remains of her pets. The priest kneeled beside her on the splintered cabin floorboards, a hand put out to support him pushed against a slippery stone slab. The flat rock fell away and clattered to one side of the broken cabin planks. His hand lodged against something soft and furry.

Donahey lifted it up out of the mist, the black fur of a sea lion pelt supple and pleasant against his fingers. In an act of compassion, he placed it over the thin-garbed sobbing shoulders of his companion.

The body next to him quit shaking. Granny placed hands palm up and rendered a final blessing, "*S dòcha an diathan agus beannaich thu lorg thu ann an nèamh.*"

Donahey crossed himself and added his own prayer.

Granny stood. "So Faither, ye hae found mah skin. All those dreary years 'n' 'twas juist below me slippers."

She started toward the beach. Donahey followed. The sea beneath the fog found their feet. He stopped and shivered as cold water flowed up his ankles. Granny rose on her toes and kissed his cheek. She pulled the skin over her head, dropped to all fours, and disappeared in the low fog. He heard some splashing. Footsteps came up behind him.

"Okay, hands on your head and turn slowly."

Donahey pulled out his dog tags, raised his arms, and pivoted.

The British Para took a long-skewed look at the jockey shorts and the shawl. "Crikey, is this what the well-dressed Argie is wearing nowadays?"

❧

Doanhey felt much better. As a prisoner of the Brits, he had been well treated. Once identified as a noncombatant, he had been turned over to the custody of the fleet navy chaplains, rather than spending time in a POW cage. The invaders had a shortage of Catholic priests. After giving his parole, the British command had pressed him into work with the medics and the gravediggers.

Today, he stood on the portside deck of Her Majesty's frigate *Antelope*. He and a Church of England priest, Reverend Charles Mayfair, had come on board to conduct services. Donahey was impressed with the ship. Although one of the smallest vessels in the invasion force, it was stuffed with over two hundred and fifty crew and armed to the teeth with cannon, torpedoes, and surface-to-surface and surface-to-air missiles. Pintle-mounted general-purpose machine guns were generously sprinkled on all the decks.

All that firepower and that of the other ships in the task force had been needed — and used — in the last few days. The Argentine air force had been busy. So far, one British ship had been sunk and four damaged.

As though his thoughts had brought them, alarms started sounding on all the ships in San Carlos. A trio of fighter-bombers came swooping in from the west, just 500 feet above the purple waters of the sound.

A smoky gray umbrella of automatic gunfire and rocket exhaust formed over the task force, the ribs of the hemisphere delineated by tracers. One fighter screamed overhead, going pell-mell for one of *Antelope's* companion ships deeper in the bay.

The plane ran into a three-dimensional space where streams of tracers merged. Giant hands pulled the aircraft to pieces. The fragments crashed into the sea. Water spouted. Donahey and Mayfair were drenched. Simultaneously, a crash and rumble from the stern of the *Antelope* made their knees shake. They grabbed each other for support.

A second crash coming from near the bow knocked them from their feet. They slid ten feet down the deck, grabbing at anything that might serve as a handhold. Donahey's feet slipped over the side. His companion seized a handful of the priest's shirt. A sailor running forward tripped and fell over Mayfair. The reverend lost his grip.

Donahey fell into the sea. He sank down, feeling the increasing pressure of the water push his clothes tight against flesh. The cold dispelled the confusion of his unexpected entry into this new dark world. He kicked and pulled with his arms. Surfacing, he gasped and received a mouthful of salt water mixed with the kerosene fuel of the downed aircraft.

Panic took hold. The priest screamed and splashed. His training took hold; he recited the Lord's Prayer. The words had a calming effect. He dog paddled as he watched the *Antelope* evade another attack and limp into the shallower arm of the bay known as San Carlos Water. Smoke rose from both bow and stern where the bombs had penetrated, but not exploded. They were either duds or had been dropped too low to arm.

A wave slapped his face, making him cough. Feet and hands became numb. He was alone. The men on the damaged ship would not have time to look for one of their lost sheep.

The needles of cold worked their way up his legs and entered his groin. He tried bobbing. Going under the water exhaling, then pushing upward to gasp a fresh lungful.

"This won't work much longer," he said aloud, desperate for a human voice, even his own. Tears formed in his eyes. His body did a half-bob, remained underwater. The light grew dim as he sank. He would breath the sea soon and it would end.

Something punched against his chest. Donahey recoiled instinctively. Sharks, already, he thought, too weak to resist.

The contact came again. It pushed him toward the surface. His face felt the sun again. He felt wet, slick fur against his neck and cheeks. A warm nose nuzzled his ear. "Keep the balance," a voice whispered.

*

The alarm rang. Donahey swam up out of the dream. He had

survived the battle. Searchers found him the next day. Seals were huddled around him, their warm bodies protection from the wind and cold.

Six Legs Good

"Okay, now draw me the hands of a clock in the nine o'clock position."

Father Ignatius Patrick Donahey pulled over the offered paper and pencil. Feeling like an idiot, he raised one eyebrow, tightened his lips, and drew a circle. From a dot in the middle, he extended out two arms one pointing straight up and one at a right angle to the left side.

"Very good. Repeat the words I gave you earlier in the examination."

With a sigh, Donahey tossed out of his memory, "Squirrel, phone, chair, bus."

Dr. Bhramini Gupta, Gerontologist, smiled and pushed back an errant lock of black hair that had come undone from her tied-back bun. Her exposed even teeth looked bleached white against dark brown skin. A paisley patterned blouse, in ambers and blacks on a khaki background, peeked from beneath her lab coat. She and her husband Shivendra, a neurologist, had immigrated to this little town in the Midwest at the same time Donahey had arrived. A lucky happenstance for him, since the community's other few doctors had full practices. Madison County Memorial Hospital, like many rural health providers, had been diligent in recruiting doctors from other countries to fill specialties short of native-born graduates.

His mind nagged him about their names. In his Jesuit

school days, they had been tasked with studying comparative religions. The Hindu surnames held religious significance, but he couldn't remember what. He would look it up later – his old university textbooks resided in a box under his bed.

The doctor's voice rose and fell in the soft, lyrical Indo-English speech of northern India. "Subject to a review of your lab tests, you are remarkably healthy. Such a condition belies the norm for your age and profession. You remain off the spirits?"

Donahey blinked. Depending upon the definition of spirits, he could give two different answers. His life since he came to Winterset had been beset by demons and wraiths: a pooka, a leprechaun, succubae, the Chinese pig god, an Aztec sun god, a hairy shape-shifter, a Native American water fiend, and a demonically possessed sentient computer.

Noting the Doctor's quizzical look, he responded, "Still on the wagon. I attend the local AA just about every day."

"What about tobacco?"

He gave a snort, "Doc, can I not have one little vice? It's apparently doing little harm."

She nodded in agreement. "Your tongue, mouth, and lungs seem free of cancer. Your PSA is within bounds. At your age, you may die of other causes before cancer manifests itself. If the blood and urine tests turn out all right, we'll mail you the results. If something of concern shows, I'll call you." Dr. Gupta took a last look at his file. "It's late August and the flu season will soon be upon us." She scribbled on a pad. "Give this to the nurse and she will administer the latest senior version of the vaccine — the first batch came in only yesterday. Guaranteed to be at least fifty percent effective. Your appointment was good timing."

Donahey's bristly brows came together, his lips pulled back, and cheeks rose to make his eyes slits. He shivered. No needles please, he thought.

The doctor chuckled, a pleasant little song coming from the back of her throat. Donahey rose, towering over her five-foot height. He opened the examination room door and found himself staring almost eye-to-eye with Dr. Gupta's nurse-enforcer, Hilda. At one hundred seventy pounds and built like a football lineman, she permitted no deviation from the doctor's orders. It was a setup. She grasped his arm and led him to the torture room.

*

The last long rays of the sun blinked behind the line of white pines forming the back boundary of the rectory lot. Donahey lay back in what was appropriately called a Stressless lounger. The heat of a ninety-five-degree day began to dissipate. A small timid breeze tickled the hairs on his arms. Crickets began their nightly castanet chorus. The swelling percussion rose to a tempo loud enough to be both heard and felt, eardrums and skin both sensitive to the vibration. Muscles relaxed, he tried to keep his mind blank – a blessed relief from the stresses of the workday and his memories of demons and death.

The flip-phone in the grass below him buzzed. A church member who had upgraded to an iPad had given Donahey the hand-me-down phone. He fumbled the cover open, irritated that this rare moment of peace had been disturbed. Damn! If it wasn't an Amber Alert. Priests and ministers of all faiths had been briefed on the program. A law enforcement agency had cause to believe that a child under the age of eighteen had been abducted and was in danger of serious bodily harm or death.

He wiped the last of the day's sweat from the corners of his eyes and squinted at the diminutive screen. The abducted was one of his own. Jennifer Davis, a seven-year-old, the only daughter of a young couple. The mother worked as a teacher at the middle school and the father, assistant manager of the local ShopKo department store. The blonde-haired second-grader had been recently enrolled in his First Communion program. Donahey pushed himself out of the recliner and rushed to find Father Brown, the full-time priest and keeper of the keys to the church pickup.

Donahey drove and Father Brown protested as they broke the speed limit and ran a red light on the way to the Davis's house. Donahey felt guilty riding in the replacement vehicle to the church's ancient Ford F-100. The old rattletrap had been totaled when it was used to crash through the chain link fence at the industrial park during his last adventure. His flirtatious nemesis, the widow Clara Murphy, had donated her deceased husband's restored 1960 Chevy El Camino. The shiny black vehicle was a cross between a sedan and a pickup.

It wasn't exactly the Batmobile, but its customized V-8 and tight racing suspension could push the vehicle up to 140 MPH. It was too powerful and too luxurious for a simple priest. However, he appreciated its capabilities today — never had he gotten across town this quickly. Peoples' faces blurred as he roared past, but he could still catch their wide-eyed looks of surprise. Squealing around a corner, he spotted the Reverend Bill Smith, the Methodist minister, leap out of the crosswalk, and reflexively make the sign of the cross. The sight gave him a mildly guilty sense of gratification.

Law enforcement vehicles, both city black-and-whites and the sheriff department's off-white cars, filled the driveway of the Davis residence. Father Brown rushed inside to comfort Jenny's parents. Donahey skipped into the backyard, where a forensic team was looking for evidence. He felt that tingly, itchy feeling which foreshadowed supernatural presence. He recognized Shawn Morgan, the sheriff's deputy.

"Father, stand back. We don't want the crime scene contaminated."

"My son, you must tell me what is going on."

Shawn pulled out a small spiral-bound notebook. "Alright, Father. Sheriff Rick is out of town to a convention, but I'm sure he would want you to be informed.

"The abduction took place at around four pm. Mother and daughter were playing in the backyard. A man leaped over the neighbor's hedge, scooped up the little girl, and hurdled the opposite fence." He pointed to the six-foot high dog-eared plank fence facing the street. "The neighbors say he ran off at high speed in a southerly direction."

"Did the intruder leave any trace?"

"Well, all we've got so far are footprints and the bare bones of a description."

Donahey moved past Shawn and knelt to examine a last footprint alongside the fence. The grass and the anchoring earth were compressed and pushed down almost two inches into the soil. It hinted that a very heavy creature had made them. Oversize odd-shaped toe impressions indicated the abductor was barefoot. He sniffed. The odor of sulfur, the old fire and brimstone kind, wafted up out of the depression. Fingers detected slime in the bottom. The grass was dead and bleached out.

A whine in his ears materialized into a yellow jacket wasp. Donahey froze. It hovered over the indentation and then flew off.

Shawn read from his notebook. "The description from the mother and the neighbor: taller than usual and bulkier. Not sure how he was clothed or if clothed at all. Dress may have been greenish. Had to be some kind of high-powered athlete to run that fast and go over barriers that high."

"Headed south, you say?"

"Yes, Father, the Iowa Highway Patrol and the sheriffs' personnel in the surrounding counties are establishing checkpoints on all roads leading out of Madison County." He glanced at his watch. "In another ten minutes we'll have the borders closed down as tight as a tick."

Donahey felt the acid in his stomach begin to rise. He felt like he would vomit. All the signs pointed to demonic kidnapping. To take an innocent was a massive breach of the rules.

The fiend was likely headed to the confluence of the ley lines that came together in Pammel Park four miles southwest of

Winterset. Ley lines formed a worldwide and inter-dimension-
al transportation system for supernatural creatures. Much of
the park's three hundred and fifty acres had been left wild, to
preserve a bit of the state's original plant diversity — perfect
camouflage for the gate.

Rising to his feet, hands absently brushed grass from his
knees. He would have to hurry. The demon had a fifteen-min-
ute head start. However, it was on foot and would have to go
cross-county over rough ground to keep from being spotted.
Even if it could run twice as fast as a human, it would still take
thirty minutes or better to reach the hidden gate. Donahey
might still have time.

Without warning, he spun and sucker-punched the unsus-
pecting deputy. Shawn tumbled to the ground. Donahey retrieved the man's pistol and raced for the church truck. He
backed down the driveway, causing an oncoming city utility
van to plough over a crab tree sapling in the Davis's front lawn.
The El Camino's tires spun, churning out black smoke.

Only a desperate man, and one guided by the hand of God,
could have managed a spontaneous slalom through the town.
Cars were pushed off the road, and stop signs ignored. The
Batmobile took to alleys and sidewalks to subvert slow vehicles, and cars stopped at intersections. Once out on county
highways the oversized V-8 pushed the fancy pickup to 120
miles per hour. The priest could feel the car lift, wanting to
go airborne.

Donahey twisted the vehicle through the park entrance going much too fast. It spun out, kicking up a choking cloud of
dust that obscured the windshield. He slapped on the wipers.
Still going too fast, he purposely sideswiped a parked Win-
nebago RV. Its wood and sheet metal side peeled off like a
snake shedding its skin, absorbing his rush. The Batmobile
bumper snapped off a wooden post marking a parking spot
and stopped. The engine rattled and died. The driver side door

was stuck. Its sheet metal looked like a huge foot with talons had kicked it in. He slipped the deputy's Glock 17 into his belt and crawled out the window.

During his days as a Chaplain in the Argentine Army, he had been familiarized with infantry weapons. Slowing to a walk on the path to the gate, he examined the pistol. Unconsecrated weapons of this world could hurt demons, but not kill them. He pulled out the magazine and placed the unloaded pistol in his belt. Drawing his pocketknife, he snapped open the short blade. He popped four of the brass nine-millimeter cartridges loose. Using the knife, he slit a cross in the head of each bullet before replacing them. After slapping the magazine back in the pistol grip, he pulled the slide back a half inch. There was an unmarked round already in the chamber.

He picked up speed, shifting from a fast walk to a jog. The gate was a quarter mile away. The parklands projected their usual beauty. Along the path, where sunbeams showed through the forest most of the day, grew purple-flowered violets. The trees on both sides consisted of multiple stands of old growth walnut with trunks several feet thick. Enough high-grade wood grew there for many years' worth of gunstocks and furniture.

He slowed to give wide berth to a pair of black mud-dabber wasps who preceded him into the glade containing the gate. Brushing aside the undergrowth, he spotted movement. The demon was green, pear-shaped, and small. Without the yellow and red flowered blouse of his hijacked victim, it would have been almost impossible to spot. The child appeared to be asleep or drugged. She hung limp, slung over the fiend's shoulders, a parody of the Shepard bringing in a lost lamb.

It spotted him and let out an "Urrk." Kidnapper and rescuer both leaped forward. The ley line gate activated in a white spiral of light. The air reeked of ozone and sulfur. It was going to be close, the priest thought. The bodies of demon and girl disappeared through the portal. Donahey made a last reflexive grab for a pointed tail.

An electric shock. He was being pulled along a mucky acidic surface. Thank God, he had attained a grip on the creature's tail. Senses stunned from the passage through the gate returned. Donahey groaned. His first perception — the smell — was a worst combination of old sweat, mold, plant rot, and excrement. His skin, the largest organ in his body, burned. Every square inch felt the acid-magma of this demon world's alien atmosphere. His eyes blinked and teared. Sight here was like looking through warped glass. Nothing felt right or fit where it should. This was a dimension operating on a radically different set of physical laws.

The gate stood open behind them. The demon dropped the child and turned to fight. It clasped him in its arms, grew a mouth and bit down on his right shoulder. The gun somehow found his hand. It fired.

The demon grunted and laughed. "No damage, Father, jus' a little 'ole."

Claws raked his back, ripping cloth and the flesh beneath. Donahey fired again — this time with a doctored bullet.

A scream. The imp leaped back. It spun on one hip, kicking and waving arms. A gaping wound began to seal. Donahey lifted the little girl, securing her with one arm against his chest and left shoulder. Reinforcements were coming. Misshapen creatures galloped, pogoed, limped, and crawled towards them. He backed towards the gate. Shouting curses, the kidnapper demon dove. Green arms spotted with random pustules tackled his legs. He fell. Half inside and half outside of the gate, Donahey pushed the pistol into the fiend's jaws and fired three times.

It convulsed. Ropy muscles writhed. The priest felt his right leg snap below the knee. He crawled backwards. A flash-jolt. Priest and child emerged into the meadow. They had made it back.

Smoke rose from their hair, clothes, and shoes. In places his trousers had been burned through, exposing blistered skin.

The girl remained asleep. Donahey was grateful. She would remember none of this. Pain shooting through his body, he fumbled for his flip phone. It was dead. The battery was as burned out as he was.

The gate remained open. He heard the flop of a heavy body. Demons armed with mis-shapen swords and spears were emerging. The gun had disappeared. In a panic, he dragged himself and the child with a leg and an arm.

A whisky-vomit voice spoke, "You won't get far that way, Father."

The tallest demon, in a human configuration, but built like a lumberjack, stepped forward and tapped his broken leg with a long-handled skeleton-headed club. Donahey grimaced and bit through his lower lip.

"What, no scream? I think we can remedy that. In the next few hours, you will be cursing God before we finish. Then you will be our meat."

"Let the child go."

The cluster of the damned roared with atonal falsetto laughter. "Father, we never intended to keep or injure the child. After all, harming an innocent is against the rules."

The priest suddenly understood. His eyebrows rose. "You mean..."

"Yas, yas, this was all a trap. An ensnarement for you."

Donahey laid the girl to one side. He crawled away. She would be out of the danger zone when they started to work on him. A swirl of dizziness came. The pain of the broken leg and the blood loss from the bite and clawed back started to send him into shock. He fought it. Wiping the back of his left hand across his mouth, he groped under his jacket for his pectoral cross.

"Now, you won't find it there. Our front man got it away from you during the scuffle. Killed him, it did. A valiant sacrifice."

The lead demon kicked him on the leg. Donahey groaned and arched his back.

"Wouldn't have done you any good. For five thousand years I worked — starving, praying, and meditating. Like your druggies becoming clean of addiction, I became clean of evil and was rewarded. But, as many of them stray back into obsession, I stray back into sin.

"In my purified state, I am protected by spells and forgiveness from receiving any hurt from creatures two or four-legged. This is why I was chosen for this job. Father, you have been too resourceful, too creative, and way too successful. Everything sent against you has been defeated, killed, or subverted."

Prayers and Bible passages rushed through Donahey's mind. A sextet of blue-winged wasps hovered over his face. The whine of insect wings grew loud. Bushes on the perimeter of the glade parted.

A honeyed, lilting voice spoke, "And so will your efforts be overcome."

Donahey saw a pair of bare feet stop at his side. He looked up brown legs to exposed wide hips and round melon breasts. The nicely stacked female assets reminded him of the smiling dance girls carved into the stone of Hindu temples. However, this female form had four arms. Her hands held weapons, a sword, mace, a trident, and a shield. The face he recognized. It was Doctor Bhramari Gupta.

"Oh, offspring of the condemned Arunasur, did you think your evil intentions were unknown?"

The devils nearest the gate shuffled their feet and took a step backwards. The boss demon inflated himself to twice his initial size, muscles popped out on thighs, arms, and legs. He laughed. "I only see two legs — no threat. Two legs bad."

Bhramari waved her multiple arms. From every point of the compass came multi-colored banners to surround and clothe her. The clouds coalesced. Flowing living points of yellow, gold, blue, and black formed a long gown from neck to ankles. Wasps, bees, and hornets in hundreds of thousands whined into the glade, their billows of multi-legged bodies so thick the sunlight dimmed.

Malformed demon bodies began to shake. Through the disrupting pain in Donahey's brain came the recollection of the story of Bhramari Devi, Goddess of Black Bees, destroyer of demons, and consort to Shiva.

The Goddess clanged her weapons together and shouted, "Six legs good."

The giant demon's body disappeared under a massive squirming swarm. He screamed. With every bee and wasp sting a cubic millimeter of him died. Hornets with their predatory mandibles tore minute bits from his flesh. The fiend was being dismantled ten thousand tiny bites a second.

Bhramari Devi tore into the secondary demons, weapons cutting off limbs, smashing heads, and impaling malformed bodies. Ineffectual repostes bounced off her shield. The demon gang broke. The gate opening was small. Panicked demons struggling to get through plugged its entrance. Goddess weapon tips became as invisible as the teeth of a buzz saw. A flood of ichor and pus flew. Donahey fainted.

*

He woke between clean sheets smelling of bleach in Madison County Memorial Hospital. Donahey smacked dry lips and mouth. Sheriff Rick dropped a copy of *Horse & Rider* magazine and walked to his side.

He offered a glass full of ice chips with a straw. Donahey took a long sip. The cool sweet liquid was as refreshing as anything he had ever tasted.

"Feeling better, Father? You should. Doctor Gupta has you shot full of antibiotics and painkillers."

"What about Jenny?'

"She's good. Back with her parents and no worse for the experience."

"And the good Doctor?"

"No damage. In fact, she seems refreshed by the experience.

She'll be checking on you when she makes her daily rounds. I wish I'd been there to see the action."

"I suppose you will be taking me into custody."

"Well, let's see, multiple counts of breaking city, county, and state traffic laws to start. Then there are damage claims for both private and public property. We can add assaulting a police officer and theft of a deadly weapon. And discharging that weapon in a public park. The Methodist minister is thinking of filing a civil suit for scaring him out of half of his allotted lifespan."

Donahey shook his head and puckered his lips. "I have a lot to pay for. I especially need to make amends to your deputy."

"Not sure it will be so bad. Shawn has already forgiven you. He said it would be a sad day when one Irishman couldn't take a punch from another. Saving a kidnapped child brings the scales of justice back into balance." The sheriff winked. "Too bad the kidnapper got away. That's what my official report says. After all, not sure the locals could handle the truth."

"Will there be jail time?"

"Probably not. I've talked to the County Attorney. She has a deal ready. Basically, you pay for all the damage and you get probation."

Donahey relaxed. Sheriff Rick's chuckle had a mischievous tinge. "I wouldn't relax too much, if I were you. The widow Clara Murphy has promised to cover whatever amount can't be raised from community donations. I'm sure she will demand a good bit of attention from you as repayment."

The Wizard and the
Queen of Demons

Father Ignatius Patrick Donahey felt like a fool. People who he thought were his friends had banded together to pressure him into this nonsense. It was Halloween.

Clara Murphy, his flirtatious nemesis, was throwing her biggest party of the season yet. Money from ticket sales made up most of the annual budget for the local Catholic Children's Foundation. Parents with children from six to fifteen years of age paid to have their progeny entertained on Beggars' Night rather than set loose on the community. When Donahey was asked to play a major role, refusing was not an option. Although, it was embarrassing and he was sure she had something else in mind.

Clara had an immense crush on him. In his long career as a priest, he'd had to deal with women being attracted to him. In spite of a few near disasters, he had managed to keep his vow of chastity.

However, Clara pushed the limits. According to the statistics, roughly fifty per cent of women her age had lost any desire for physical relations, another thirty per cent felt an occasional rare itch needing to be scratched, and the remainder retained the sex drive of their youth. Clara's libido had clawed its way to the top one percent of the last group.

Her plan to get him thoroughly involved — and possibly vulnerable — had worked. His broken leg from a year ago had healed to the point where it couldn't be used as an excuse to say no. She had stolen this year's party theme from Tolkien's *Lord of the Rings*. Outfitted as Gandalf the Grey, he stood on the porch of her massive three-story turreted Victorian house greeting the other arrivals.

Some fifty children had been dropped off, a sizeable percentage of Winterset's preteen young folk. Miniature hobbits, elves, dwarves, and orcs had raced up a sidewalk bounded by a dozen lighted Jack O' Lanterns. Candlelight shining through their sharp-carved teeth cast fang-like patterns on the concrete. Farther back on both sides leafless skeletal trees with the exception of a seventy-foot tall pin oak seemed to reach out at passersby. The total effect was suitably eerie.

Clara had spent much time and money on his costume. The long robes, sewn of thick gray wool, besides being heavy, itched where they touched back and chest. Fake hair spirit-glued on by one of the local amateur players formed white bangs, mustache, and beard. A wide-brimmed pointy hat and felt slippers with soles too thin to be comfortable completed the outfit.

He felt overheated in the whole weighty mess. Since the robe hung down to his ankles, he decided to wear only a pair of underwear underneath. The only part he liked was the long oak staff, although he had to restrain himself from smacking some of the wiseacre adult guests with it.

The last of the invitees flowed in. His psychologist and resident witch, Dr. Catherine Darcy, strode up the sidewalk with a creak of leather and rasp of metal. Like a number of the citizens of Winterset, Iowa, she led a double life. An innocuous professional personality on the outside hid the mind and capabilities of an ageless preternatural creature.

There were others, a former leprechaun, and now part owner of the local winery. The physician, Dr. Bhramini Gupta, saving lives and curing sickness of local mortals, yet capable of transforming into the Indian Goddess of Black Bees, destroyer of demons and consort to Shiva. Even the county sheriff possessed the secret identity of an Irish pooka, a shape-shifter able to turn into a coal-black horse at need.

Moreover, these were his allies. He shuddered, remembering the number of truly evil manifestations he and his associates had disposed of to date. Donahey didn't want to think about it, but there were probably other secret creatures, good and bad, hiding behind the smiling everyday faces of neighbors and parishioners.

It was the ley lines, of course. Those invisible channels of supernatural power covered the earth. In special places they came together to form gateways, one of which was located in the heavily wooded state park south of Winterset. Donahey initially thought he had come to this place of his own free will to retire in the sixtieth year of his career as a Catholic priest. Quickly disabused of that notion, he found himself cast as guardian of the gate.

Cat Darcy's approach broke the chain of his thoughts. Costumed head-to-foot in armor, she pulled off a Viking-style helmet, allowing long golden locks to cascade down. She raised an arm in mock salute.

"I am Éowyn, niece of Théoden, King of Rohan, and destroyer of the Witch-king of the Nazgûl. I salute you, Gandalf."

There was someone missing. A black shadow fluttered down from above and thumped on his shoulder. He jumped and frowned, then smiled. Corbeau, a heavyweight crow, her familiar, half-spread his wings, opened his beak, and cackled. It sounded like the peals of demonic laughter produced by early movie villains. The crow had picked it up from watching late night TV.

The bird pecked at his false white locks, shook its wings, and said "Booger."

Donahey pulled a small piece of hamburger from his pocket, striped off the plastic wrap, and handed the meat over. It formed a bulge in the bird's black-feathered throat as it gulped the treat.

"So, Father, who's present tonight?"

"You and I, and Blair, the former leprechaun, now attired as Golum. Dr. Brahimi is at a convention at Johns Hopkins and the sheriff is prowling the town and county to keep the older teens from destroying civilization as we know it. Clara is inside with Father Brown leading games and passing out candy and cookies."

"Let's take a look."

The fancy-carved screen door closed behind them with a bang. They walked down the entry hall. Donahey stopped to examine a baseball bat positioned on two padded hooks on the wall next to the library door. Centered over it hung a framed eight-by-ten black and white photograph of a ball team. He looked closer; the players wore old-fashioned uniforms with three-quarter sleeves, long socks, and pants tied off below the knees. A hand grasped his forearm. The hostess had appeared.

Clara raised a hand. "That's a picture of the New York Yankees. The man here," she pointed, "is George Herman Ruth, Jr., also known as Babe Ruth, 'the Bambino' or 'the Sultan of Swat.' Over here on the end, the one with the buckteeth, that's my grandfather. He was one of the team's batboys."

Donahey knew baseball well. One of his first assignments had been to the Cathedral of the Virgin Mary of the Immaculate Conception in Havana, Cuba, a hotbed of baseball aficionados. He had learned the game and attended many playoffs. A year later, the Archbishop and one hundred fifty priests — he among them — had been kicked off the island by Castro.

He took a closer look at the bat. The age-darkened wood had a few dings and a column of eyelash-shaped notches.

Clara provided background, "It's a 1927 hickory Louisville slugger weighing forty-two ounces and running thirty-six inches long with a medium handle and a medium barrel."

"May I touch it?"

She squeezed his arm. "Certainly."

Donahey ran his fingers over the sweat-stained wood. He felt the nicks.

"Babe carved those notches to mark twenty-one of the sixty home runs he hit that season. And it holds a secret passed down to me from Grandfather."

Fascinated, Donahey stared at the antique. "And what is that?"

Clara turned slightly, leaned in closer, and pushed one breast into his shoulder. "Like many athletes, Babe was superstitious. At his request, grandfather secretly took this bat to the main cathedral in every city in which they played to have it blessed by the local priests."

Donahey felt the softness of the largish breast through his costume. He began to sweat. He wondered what stratagem he could use to counter Clara's unwanted intimacy.

She continued her recitation. "Multiple blessings and sprinkling of holy water were received that season in New York, Boston, Chicago, Washington, Detroit, St. Louis, and Cleveland."

Donahey nodded. Not only a revered artifact of a baseball legend, it had become a holy relic as well. A pint-sized orc burst out of the parlor door, grabbing at a laughing elf. Clara ran in chase. All games and nonsense were to be confined to the twin parlors, now connected through the opening of double sliding pocket doors.

The shouts and buzz of fifty kids and their supervising adults diminished to a dull roar as Cat Darcy closed the hall-way entries to the parlors. She sidled over. On her right shoulder, Corbeau hung on and tried to look wise.

"Sheriff Rick asked me to brief you on the latest mystery."

"You mean the strange deaths of four men, all occurring in a three-day period? I heard it was a rash of heart attacks."

"He thinks they are suspicious, too many, too close together. You link the locations by time of death — connect the dots —

and you find a path from the ley lines' gate to the city."

"Has something come through? And in time for Halloween, the night when bad things have more power. I hope it's not tonight. I left my cross, Bible, and holy water back at the rectory."

"There's likely a family Bible in the library."

The screen door rattled. A cold wind blew. Strained through the wire mesh it gave off discordant notes, like stones hitting ill-tuned harp strings. Donahey felt an itchy, tingly feeling which surpassed the itch from the wool clothing. Priest and witch ran to the entrance.

They sneezed and held their breath. The smells of sulfur and rot like that of bloated corpses blew over them, impregnating their clothes and leaving an oily residue on exposed skin.

Hand over mouth, eyes wide, Cat hissed, "The Night Hag comes."

Donahey gasped. A woman stood on the city sidewalk near the curb. She was not the picture of what one expected in a middle-class Midwest small town. Below long arched eyebrows, separated by a thin Roman nose, wide ice-colored eyes stared from dark sockets. Purple-tinged white hair hung in tatters down both sides of a lean face. It glowed with dangerous beauty.

The body was naked and bestowed with fertile female curves. The feet gave away her bestiality. They stretched out more than a foot and a half, eight toes extended three to six inches and ended in curved tiger claws. Residual dewclaws sprouted half way up her calves.

A racking shudder ran through Donahey's body. He was both instinctively attracted and strongly repelled by her. The apparition could only be one thing.

The answer came from his companion, "Lilith, Queen of demons — the first unfaithful wife of Adam. The begetter of demons, seducer/destroyer of men, and the abductor of their children."

Donahey recited a part of Proverbs:

"...who has forsaken the partner of her youth and forgotten the covenant of her God; for her house is the way down to death, and her course leads to the land of the dead. None who resort to her find their way back or regain the path to life."

The mystery of the four dead men was solved. Lilith ignored them and stared through the front windows at the children playing inside.

Cat shouted, "Damn, she's here for the kids!" and snapped her two arms forward.

The iron gate at the entrance slammed shut. The old house still possessed a six-foot tall wrought iron fence marking the boundary of its lot. Consisting of upright rods tipped with spear points, it should provide a barrier to supernatural creatures, which couldn't stand the touch of the metal.

A second wave of the good witch's hands and the curtains in the front façade's floor-to-ceiling windows slid shut. The children and their chaperones couldn't see out and Lilith couldn't see in. Donahey heard Cat chant a short garble of what sounded to him like nonsense syllables. The copper mesh in the screens on door and windows glowed silver. His psychologist witch was casting defensive spells.

"Be prepared to fight, Father, this won't be enough to stop her."

Donahey gulped and raised his staff. Outside, Lilith lifted a leg and slammed it down. The concrete sidewalk leading up to the house cracked down the middle and lifted three feet off the ground. The Jack O' Lanterns on both sides turned to orange mush, their lights extinguished. The gate blew off its hinges. The Demon woman swooped into the yard.

The screech of tires and a flashing light bar announced the arrival of a patrol car doing a high-speed turn. It accelerated down the street, crashed through the fence, pushed aside bushes, and knocked over a young pine tree.

Lilith turned. She froze in the headlights, like a jacklighted rabbit. The steel push bumper welded to the vehicle front scooped her up with a bang. The car bounced over the lawn barely slowing. The front end crashed into the massive pin oak. A blizzard of scarlet and bronze leaves swirled around the base of the tree, like a shook-up snow globe.

The leaves settled. Cat and Donahey could see a struggling Lilith trapped between the car bumper and tree, pinned like a beetle on a display board. Booted feet kicked out the spider-webbed front windshield. A uniformed man they recognized as Sheriff Rick crawled out. Lilith hissed. She pushed. The patrol car shifted with a groan of metal.

Rick stripped off his shoes, shirt, and pants. He shape-shifted into his pooka alter ego, a coal black horse. It reared. A sheet of flame blew out of its mouth and nostrils. Lilith screamed and writhed. The remaining dry fall leaves on the oak caught fire. Like a giant torch, it lit up the entire block. The demon bitch lifted her arms. The car jerked back and flipped on its side.

Now free, Lilith leaped. Hanging onto the horse's neck, she twisted. The pooka fell. Donahey shouted. Cat gasped and made mystic passes. Lilith lifted and raised the horse over her head. Tree roots began to writhe and wrapped themselves around the fiend up to her waist.

She tossed the pooka. Sailing through the air, it smacked into a Norwegian spruce and slid down unconscious. Lilith tore away the roots. Cat gasped and began to sweat. Each spell she had cast left a path. Lilith pushed her venom down their back trails.

The silver protective glow on the screens blew out like a candle flame in a thunderstorm. Cat took the full brunt of a curse. Her eyes rolled up in her head. The witch's body jerked, spread arms and legs, and collapsed. Corbeau fell over like a bird electrocuted on a power line.

The screen door crashed open. Donahey felt the anger of his Irish ancestors flash through his veins. He raised his staff and shouted the ancient war cry of his clan, *"Farrah Cromaboo!"*

The Queen of Demons danced forward, fangs displayed, and eyebrows lifted.

"You shall not have the children." Donahey swung the staff.

Lilith's hand grabbed and twisted. The staff shattered. She pulled him close and whispered. "I came for you. But now I think I'll take the children too."

"In the name of –"

Her hand went over his mouth and sealed it. He couldn't invoke the Trinity. An electric shock wave pulse blazed through his body. Every nerve synapse closed. Every muscle contracted. His fingers and toes curled. Breath shushed out. His heart stopped.

Pain, so intense it blinded him, flooded his every atom. Donahey wanted to scream. Nothing came out. The paralysis ceased. He filled his lungs. The night hag's odor choked him, rotten meat, excrement, mold, decaying skin... His heart restarted.

"So, my little wizard, my lover, let me pretty myself for thee."

He shuddered as black buboes formed on the side of her head and neck. She grinned. They broke open. Yellow pus ran down. He struggled, attempted a head-butt.

A second high-voltage surge daggered into him. His body froze. Lungs and heart stopped again. One minute dragged by, then another. He was suffocating and having a heart attack simultaneously.

Lilith brought him back. "Yes. Keep fighting. I will break you. We have an eternity."

She adjusted her arms to hug him close to her body. A foot-long red-crusted tongue snaked out of her scabbed lips. It laved along his neck and up under his chin. Without his consent, he felt his maleness respond.

Looking over the demon's shoulder, Donahey spotted Clara. She opened the door of the first parlor and entered the hallway with a tray of glasses. She must be headed to the kitchen for refills. Music and the chatter of children at play flooded the scene. The partiers remained unaware of how close they were to disaster. Closing the door behind her, returned the hall to silence. Clara turned.

The mistress of the house spotted Cat crumpled unconscious on the floor. She almost dropped the tray. Clara's face turned red as she took in Donahey and the Queen of Demons in what looked like the foreplay preceding sexual congress. The priest could see her anger and jealousy rising.

Clara crouched. Her eyes narrowed. Lips grew thin. She wasn't about to let someone else take her prize. She threw the tray and glasses and rushed forward. Donahey tried to warn her. His spell-sealed lips remained closed. Clara stood no chance against Lilith. He closed his eyes and prayed internally.

Donahey felt a shock. Lilith's embrace loosened. He felt another shock. The demon woman dropped him. He hit the floor like a frozen side of beef. He tried to speak. Tried to rise.

He couldn't believe what he saw. Clara had grabbed the closest weapon. Her first two blows had caused the demon to release him.

The Babe Ruth bat smacked Lilith in the shoulder. Left arm raised to protect her from the blows of a many-times-blessed holy relic, the Queen of Demons stumbled down the hallway and out the front door. A berserk Clara continued to attack. The bitch queen's head bled purple ichor from strikes to the forehead and jaw. The right arm hung limp. Bright red bruises covered her ribs and buttocks.

Clara's Irish was up. The bat was a blur. It made the crack sound of a home run every time it connected. Lilith fell off the front porch onto the broken concrete. She leaped up and ran for the gate. Clara smacked her twice more, before stopping the chase at the entrance to her property. With two hands, she raised the bat over her head and gave it a victory shake.

Two fire trucks pulled up. Yellow-coated men and women hustled hoses in through the gate and began to fight the pin oak blaze, which had spread to the surrounding trees and the patrol car. A red-faced Sheriff Rick staggered into the house. His naked body was covered only by his uniform shirt tied around his waist, his remaining clothes consumed in the fire. He looked at Clara still holding the bat and glanced out the door at a limping pinpoint glow from the retreating Queen of Demons.

"Girl, you sure banged that one out of the park."

Clara kneeled near Donahey, who still paralyzed lay with his torn gray robe bunched above his waist. She looked, grimaced, and said, "Oh my, Patrick, what a big stiffie you have."

Donahey sat alone in the front row pew of the church. He prayed he might live down the embarrassment of two nights ago. They had all survived. Sheriff Rick had some cracked ribs and a possible concussion. Cat Darcy was due to be re-leased from the hospital tomorrow. The local medical folks had misdiagnosed her condition as a mild stroke. A recovered Corbeau lived in temporary quarters with him in the rectory. He liked the crow, but it had terrible tastes in TV programs. Binge-watching soap operas caused it to moan and groan. In the evenings, it focused on old black-and-white horror movies where it greeted the entrance of the villain with shaking half-opened wings and cackles. Getting the bird back to its bound companion would be a relief.

All the children had been saved with no trauma. With the drapes and doors closed, none of the innocents in the parlors had the slightest idea of what had transpired. Donahey shud-dered. No thought of how close they had come to....

He had escaped with the least physical damage — sore mus-cles and a temporary heart arrhythmia. Clara was acting like a wife who had caught her husband cheating. Of course, it was impossible to tell her the truth. He was grateful she had sur-prised the Queen of Demons and chased her off. In a few more minutes, Donahey would have lost his immortal soul.

It couldn't be explained to Clara, so he remained high up on her bad list. He guessed that condition wouldn't last long, especially since she had discovered first hand that even at his age, he could still get it up. He would enjoy the lack of her attention, if only for a little while.

Officially, the whole episode was attributed to Halloween vandals, although no one had figured out how the concrete sidewalk had been uprooted.

Pixies, a Troll, and a ...

Father Donahey, in blue-striped pajamas and ancient checked wool flannel robe, sat in a bentwood rocker in the rectory's screened-in back porch. A gentle breeze murmured through the netting bringing the mixed aroma of lilac, azalea, and peonies. He glanced out at the backyard's profusion of flowers and plants. Two years ago, a volunteer committee of church members decided the three-quarter acre plot of grass, weeds, and broken glass must be upgraded.

A specialist in garden design from Iowa State University's Reiman Gardens produced a plan. Yellow brick pathways snaked through and around Oz-themed plantings. Strategically placed rags-and-straw scarecrow, stone lion, and rusty tin man metal sculpture waited for a Dorothy to give them purpose. Wicked witch legs carved from ebony logs sheathed in striped stockings poked out from under the potting shed foundation. On its granite-colored crenellated roof posed a flying monkey whirligig, its wings a spinning, buzzing blur. The committee had challenged wood carvers throughout the state to submit entries in a 'good witch' contest, the winning submission to be placed in the tennis court-size poppy field.

While not much of a gardener, Donahey had to admire the result. The magnificent blues, yellows, reds, and emerald greens were matched by a perfume which even his seventy-three-year-old nose could detect and appreciate. He listened to the underlying collective sound of the plot — half buzz, half whisper. Today, an insect kaleidoscope of tints and shades, nature's color wheel, danced over the grounds. Many of the plants had been chosen to attract pollinators and butterflies

He smiled. The dwarf apple tree clusters, curvaceous beds of poppies, columbine, asters, Griffith Buck roses, and many other annuals and perennials had attracted more than just beneficial insects. He was also sure that a horde of *Pobel Vian*, known in English as pixies, had made the place home. The first signs came a year ago, when strange four-inch long fliers kept popping in and out of his peripheral vision. When he looked directly at the area, nothing appeared. The other signs he remembered from his grandfather's tales in Ireland were dance rings of trampled grass, mushrooms springing up overnight, and the supernatural lushness of the plant growth. The old man had quoted him a fragment of a poem by Samuel Minturn Peck:

'Tis said their forms are tiny, yet
All human ills they can subdue,
Or with a wand or amulet
Can win a maiden's heart for you;
And many a blessing know to stew
To make your wedlock bright;
Give honor to the dainty crew,
The Pixies are abroad tonight.

Donahey tried to stay on the Little Peoples' good side. Following his Daideó's practice, he had left bowls of unseparated milk, top-heavy with cream, on the back steps. The priest had also risked getting a sissy-reputation, buying Barbie doll clothes at garage sales. Left overnight, the gifts disappeared by dawn. They would be a bit too large for the finger-long pixies, but he felt sure they could tailor them. Donahey believed they were pleased with his efforts, as he had not had a cold for over two years and the pain in his ancient knees had miraculously vanished. In addition, they kept cats out of the yard, which included Clara Murphy's attack cat, Tiger. Unfortunately, they displayed no desire to keep the blasted feline's mistress away — an impossibility anyway, since she was also chairperson of the church garden committee.

Donahey took a sip of heavily sugared coffee and reflected upon his state of mind, body, and clothing. The pajama top had a hole in the left elbow and frayed cuffs, but through repeated washings over the last ten years had become much too soft and comfortable to discard. The robe was almost as old, its age disclosed by shiny fabric on the butt and elbows. If clothes could be old friends, these garments qualified. As he lived alone, no one except the laundress had any idea of the state of his wardrobe, and bless her, she wasn't talking.

A curl of smoke rose from the pipe on the side table. His physician and his psychologist both were trying to break him of smoking. Their latest attempt came from a tobacco mix they had formulated. It wouldn't hurt his lungs, they claimed. Barely smokable, it had a pastel-pink, putty-like consistency with an odor no respectable tobacco plant would produce. Mostly it consisted of a strong peppermint scent and flavor to the tongue that failed to hide an aftertaste similar to old ground up athletic socks. It was all he was allowed. In a weak moment, he had promised to use the face-bittering blend.

Of course, they, Dr. Bhramari Gupta and Dr. Catherine Darcy, never personally experienced the depths of human weakness, mostly since they weren't human. The first being an immortal Hindu wasp goddess, and the second the younger sister of Joan of Arc and a witch on the European model. Father Donahey realized they were trying to help him both personally and with the mission. However, it wasn't like he had volunteered for this work.

The church hierarchy had also played a deceptive role. Supposedly, he was Winterset, Iowa's retired priest, only helping when full-time Father Brown was ill or out of town. It wasn't the life of books and long rural walks he had expected. The community and the surrounding area were awash with supernatural creatures. Some friendly, some not, but all had to be dealt with in order to protect his new parish, state, country, and the wider world from chaos and destruction. The mantle of guardian had been forced upon him.

The last six months had been free of major paranormal intrusion, except for a brief scare. Sheriff Rick had shared with him suspicious sightings of a homeless person who had established residence under the one hundred-and-six-foot-long Hogback Covered Bridge, spanning the North River on Douglas Township Road. Farmers along the waterway began to report livestock mutilations — something was killing cattle and eating on the carcasses.

The lawman possessed a special sixth sense when it came to awareness of mythical creatures. The man himself, being another denizen of the Madison County supernatural scene, lived the secret life of a shape-shifting Irish wraith. The mischievous and destructive nature of his demon personality was kept in check by his oath of office. He would serve and protect the citizens of this county as long as the vow remained in effect. Donahey shuddered to think of what might happen if Rick was defeated in an election and released from his bond.

Waiting for a dark night, the two of them had set up a stakeout near the bridge. After letting the night settle around them, the sheriff slipped out of his clothes and transformed into his favorite pooka-shape, a coal-black stallion. He would be the bait, while the Father crept behind with a net and the Sheriff Department's taser gun.

Lightning bugs flashed from air and grass tips, males aloft, and females signaling below. Crickets played raspy leg violins. In horse-mode, Rick casually grazed his way up to the riverbank. Head lowered to guzzle cool water; he became as vulnerable as all herd animals when drinking.

A rush of water and a dark amorphous body exploded out of the riverbed. Long arms grasped the pooka's neck. Moonlight reflected off a pair of long off-white tushes.

With a speed unexpected of a normal equine, the pooka reared and twisted its neck. The attacking creature's jaws missed and shut with the sound of a screen door slamming. Muscles convulsed, the horse's chest and head flew back. Missing its prey and off balance, the attacker spiraled into a somersault. Its heavy body smacked into the earth, well away from the river.

A startled Father Donahey fired the taser into the right buttock of the black stallion. It grunted, quivered, and fell to its knees. Face forming a guilty grimace, the priest spit out his favorite cuss word, "Cornflakes!"

He tossed the net. This time he ensnared the correct victim. The creature squealed and rolled, almost throwing off the web of one-inch diameter polyethylene rope. Donahey leaped and hugged the being's pillow-sized hips, keeping it from escaping. It tossed and writhed.

Water squeezed out of its body hair soaked the priest's clothes. The smell of rusty river bottom, aged fish slime, and bad carnivore breath washed over him. He hoped he could hold on long enough for the sheriff to recuperate.

Arms became numb and aching. His grip slipped. A heavy unclothed human-scale body bumped next to him. The sheriff had recovered in time, grabbing the creature around the chest. He twitched and swore, discovering it had breasts. It let out a recognizable female scream.

Father Donahey chuckled. "I think she has misinterpreted the intent of your naked attack. Now to be sure, I won't be telling anyone about this, if you won't be telling anyone about my bad aim."

*

The two women doctors had taken the subdued prisoner in hand. After an examination, they reported the creature to be a

169

thousand-year-old six-foot tall female troll. One of the north-ern Scandinavian Huldrefolk variety, she possessed a more human-like body and features than the southern Germanic breed. The exceptions were upper and lower three-inch long self-sharpening tushes hidden behind thick lips, the muscular development of a weight lifter, waterproof fur, and a four-foot long tail. The face, hands, and feet were free of hair. The ears were small and held back against the head — like most aquatic animals — and the size of the nose large, but within the range of human features. A shave here and there, a dress to hide the tail, better language skills, and coaching on manners, and she could pass as human.

After deciding the troll couldn't be turned loose to prey on the local livestock, and possibly humans, as the old stories about her kind hinted, the group placed her as housekeeper to the rectory. Here, in this reasonably private household, she would learn more English and social skills. Her name in the garbled ancient Norwegian she spoke, translated to Thorn Bush, so they named her Rose. Given her need for large quan-tities of raw meat, they received an on-going grant from FIB-MC, the Foursquare Institute for the Benefit of Mythological Creatures.

Father Donahey had not been pleased with the decision. He was not cut out to be a Professor Higgins, as in *My Fair Lady*. Oh, he could add to her small store of English, and he was irascible enough. But, his life-long church-imposed bachelor-hood had not prepared him to present solutions to women's intimate concerns. He had extracted ironclad promises from the doctors to handle that part. However, they had all agreed to see how well she adapted and if there might be a place for her in human society.

The last four months had passed with Rose making great strides. Bright and adaptable, she quickly gained proficiency in language and manners. Her female counselors had excitedly arranged visits to the hairstylist, cosmetician, and shopping trips to West Des Moines' Jordan Creek Mall. The women, as excited as if it was Christmas, hauled in packages containing plus-size fashions from Chicos, GAP, Old Navy, Talbots, and even Victoria's Secret.

Father Donahey clicked his tongue and shook his head. The doctors had reverted to their doll-playing childhoods. Rose entered, dressed in a flower-print calf-length day dress. She offered a tray holding a plate of sugar cookies, coffee pot, and sugar and creamer. He noted she had shaved her legs.

"More coffee, Father?"

≈

Donahey was worried. He paced back and forth in front of the parlor's double-hung windows. The ancient grandfather clock in the entryway had struck ten and yet no sign of Rose. Her still-made bed was proof she had been out all night. He looked at the rectory phone posed on its oak Craftsman table. He picked up the receiver, wondering which of the doctors he should call first.

A car door slammed. Replacing the phone, he pulled the drapes aside. Walking up the sidewalk came Rose, escorted by Sheriff Rick. A sense of relief and then one of disaster washed over him. He rushed to the door and pulled it open.

The sheriff waved. "Not to worry, she's all right."

Rose entered, wearing blue jeans, a long-sleeved beige western shirt, and a modern take-off on cowboy boots. The outfit was wrinkled. Mud coated the boots and stained the trousers up to the knees.

Donahey looked her up and down. She blushed and bowed her head. "My child, where have — ?"

Sheriff Rick interrupted. "Rose, you go get cleaned up, I'll talk with the Father."

Given an out, the troll-woman sped off up the stairs. The two men walked through the house and into the privacy of the garden. They strolled down the yellow brick road.

"Well, the good news is that our girl can party."

Donahey's eyebrows went up. He raised a hand in a questioning gesture.

"Here's the story. I received a call of an altercation at The Cycle Shop, you know, the bikers' bar out at the old Swensen place. When I arrived, a concerned Knut Helgesen, relayed the events. He had met Rose in the checkout lane at the Fairway Tuesday, engaged her in conversation and asked her out to celebrate hump day with him."

Donahey was shocked. His Rose dating a Lutheran. Then reality set in. Rose wasn't Catholic and couldn't be a member of any religious group in her current demonic state. She couldn't even enter consecrated ground. Besides, he could see the attraction. Knut was one of Madison County's four hundred and fifty Norwegian-Americans. A Wegian troll would feel at home in that group.

"At any rate, they rode his custom Harley out to the road house last night to meet with his group, the Thor's Hammers. After several hours of drinking and dancing, a rival biker gang showed up. It didn't take long before bad blood between the two bands degenerated into violence."

Donahey grimaced. "She didn't...?"

"Use the tushes? No, just fists, elbows, knees, and feet. Knut tried to push her down behind the bar. With a whoop and a roar, she leapt into the knots of struggling men, and without regard to sides started laying them out."

Grabbing the sheriff's arm, Donahey choked out, "Any serious casualties?"

"The worst, a broken jaw, but there were plenty of black eyes, bruises, and cracked ribs." Rick laughed, "And, a whole lot of admiration. Those old boys hadn't seen the like. It was the most fun they'd had in ages. So no charges were pressed, and Rose was made an honorary member of each gang. However, the owner wants reimbursed for the damage to chairs, tables, pool table, light fixtures, plasterboard, ceiling tiles, etc., etc."

Donahey looked back at the rectory. "What about Rose?"

"She had fled the scene, afraid her true nature would be revealed. I picked her up just two hours ago on a gravel farm-to-market road just off County 34. No apparent damage, except for scraped knuckles."

"And the bottom line is..."

With a chuckle Rick responded, "Well, there are about fifty guys that desperately want to date her. They'll be a plague on your house."

The two men walked past the potting shed/castle. The flying monkey whirligig spun its wings, buzzed, and turned to face the wind. Donahey started to return to the rectory. The sheriff grasped his arm and guided him further down the path.

"On a serious note, there is something else that may involve our charge. The cattle mutilations have begun again. And worse."

Donahey felt the sheriff's fingers squeeze his elbow. "A body has been robbed from a private cemetery up county. Has Rose been out at night?"

The pixies were all aflutter. He could feel it. They had ignored the cream and milk offering left last night. Donahey stood on the yellow brick path where it curved around the back of the garden. Shadows grew as the sun dropped below the earth's curvature. The growing darkness made it difficult to observe details. He examined a large patch of coneflowers and daisies, roughly five feet by five feet, which lay blackened and twisted. Flowers on the edges of this dead zone had lost their nearest petals and leaves. It looked like someone had sprayed herbicide or even a deadly burst of radiation.

Donahey's nostrils flared. The smell was foul. It was worse than the time he had helped Granny Wilson's son break into her house to discover she had died in a hot kitchen three days earlier – two burners on her gas stove still firing.

Someone or something had invaded the garden and waited in this patch to observe. The last months had been too peaceful. Perhaps another malevolent manifestation had arrived. Sheriff Rick and a deputy had stopped by an hour ago to take Rose in for questioning. Trolls had a modus operandi which could include cattle killings and body snatching. He couldn't believe she was the perp.

Before they ushered her out, she had whispered to him, "Father, something bad is coming. Let me stay."

He wondered if he had done right by letting them take her. At least, he thought, I should have gone with her. A decision came. He would get the old bicycle out of the garage, pump up its tires, and pedal down to the jail.

He turned. Something rustled in the bushes. A buzzing, whining noise assaulted his ears. Tiny voices sang a one-word chorus, "Run!" They weren't mosquitoes. He took the pixies' advice. His leather-soled shoes slapped the brick walkway in rapid sequence. A half moon and multitudes of stars lit his path.

He had never been a good runner and legs over seven decades old rendered him even slower. Donahey raced past the tin man sculpture and drew level with the poppy field. His lungs began to labor. A huge shadow-creature hurdled out of the undergrowth and slammed into him.

The upper bone in his right arm cracked. The Father sailed ten feet face down into the poppies. He shook. His attacker advanced. The shape against the moonlight was hunched over; long arms with grasping hands connected to a massive chest. Fingers flashed down tearing through the cloth of his trousers and cutting the flesh of his calf. The pain broke his frozen panic. He crawled away on his side, unbroken arm and legs pulling and pushing. The pursuit would be short.

The creature — could it be Rose or another troll? — bounded up and cocked an arm. The smell of rotting meat and grave dirt washed over him. Hooked fingers with six-inch talons descended. Father Donahey tried to close his eyes and failed. A flash of silver intercepted the arm. Three fingers leapt off the demon's hand and spun off into the darkness.

The creature screamed and recoiled. The tin man raised his axe and chopped. This time a pointed ear flew off the side of a beast-like head. The monster hugged the tin man. They went down together in a crash of metal. The demon beat on the animated metal, making drum sounds, at first bass and then collapsing to tenor and the high-pitched screech of tearing sheet metal.

It came to Donahey. The pixies, the pixies were defending their territory. Their magic had animated the sculpture. He started to crawl again. If he could get deep into the field and stay low, the dense four-foot tall poppies might hide him.

The thing finished off the tin man and sucked on the stumps of its severed fingers. It howled and bounded after Donahey. It seemed as though it would catch him. Snake-like, something squirmed out of the flowers and wrapped itself around the fiend's legs. The monster tripped and fell. Rolling on its back, it kicked upward. Donahey spotted rags and straw tied around its ankles. The scarecrow had made its attack. He began to crawl again.

The demon bent down and tore at the entangling mess with its remaining talons and a mouthful of razor-edged teeth. Dorothy's first friend was shredded into scraps.

Donahey came to the end of the poppy field and rolled out onto the yellow brick road. He managed to gain his feet and stumble towards the house. He heard the scrape of the demon's toenails against brick. It lunged. Donahey shouted and fell. Bounding out from under the apple trees, a four-legged beast smacked the fiend with a paw and closed jaws around its thigh. The not-so-cowardly lion had arrived.

The pair rolled and roared. With all the noise, Donahey wondered why the whole neighborhood wasn't awake. The monster raised hands and repeatedly smashed them against the back half of the cat. It was only concrete. Under the preternaturally strong blows it cracked in half. The jaws remained, biting and chewing the creature's thigh until that piece also broke into fragments.

Donahey pushed up and crawled on one hand and knees. The demon limped after him, dark ichor flowing from its wounds on hand and leg. The priest glanced over his shoulder. The thing was still faster than him.

It tripped. Something close to invisible kicked it in the jaw. He heard bone break. The demon tried to stand. Something kicked it in the behind. It grabbed its buttocks. Donahey caught a glimpse of black legs from the knees down. The witch's legs from under the potting shed had charged. The tough ebony wood bruised flesh and broke bones. Undaunted the demon grabbed one of the magicked legs and used it like a club to demolish the other. It tossed the splintered remains to one side. Whining and groaning, it rubbed its wounds and cuts.

It spotted Donahey lying exhausted twenty feet away. Now the priest knew. It was another assassin come to remove him from his too successful guardian role. He began to pray. The fiend limped up to him and leaned over. Drool dribbled onto the priest's face. Icy hands secured his neck and began to squeeze.

Donahey heard a whizzing, buzzing sound. Something smacked into the demon's face. The flying monkey darted in with pixies on its back. The little people flung thorn-tipped spears. The fiend's hands released Donahey's neck to defend itself. The monkey made more passes. The creature from hell stood to gain more height.

A six-foot long hairy body crashed into the monster. Donahey recognized Rose's new perfume. She was back! The two forms rolled together. Donahey tried to compute the odds. The fiend-assassin was larger and more heavily muscled. But it was hurt and couldn't use its teeth with a broken jaw. The fight would be equal, the odds only fifty-fifty.

The demon lifted Rose and slammed her down on the brick. She was stunned. He used the talons on his feet to cut her belly. The monkey whirligig flew in to crash against the fiend's face. A splinter entered its left eye. It grabbed the two pixie riders and squeezed them. Fragile bones and organs turned into mush.

It raised its head in triumph. From its now blind side, Rose pushed through its defenses. Her tushes closed on its neck and bit out its throat. A second bite cut through its spine. The monster collapsed. Rose knelt beside Donahey and checked his body for wounds.

"You'll be all right, Father. The sheriff will be here shortly. I only came back to say goodbye."

Donahey tried to convince himself to argue her to stay, but all that came out of his confused brain was "Bless you, my child."

Tears ran down his cheeks. He collapsed into darkness. The last thing he remembered was hearing Rose dragging away the monster's body.

❦

Father Donahey sat once again in the rocker on the rectory back porch. A coffee cup sat on the side table. A pipe rode in his mouth and one arm rested in a sling.

"Could you not smoke that nasty stuff when I'm about?" Sheriff Rick said.

"Well now, if you would finish your business you could leave at any time."

Donahey remained in a bad mood; the drugs prescribed had only dulled his battle wounds. And of course, the sheriff was right; the tobacco was awful.

"All right. I mentioned that Rose had escaped our custody and arrived back at the house in time to rescue you. Fortunately, the pixies had damaged your attacker quite a bit before she intervened."

"Did you find out what it was?"

"Yes, we found a few gnawed bones and scraps of flesh a mile or two north in the Miller's stand of walnut trees. Rose had evidently eaten him for trail rations."

Donahey shivered. "Go on."

"The doctors and I are convinced it was a ghoul, an eater of humans, whether alive or dead. These fiends are armed with long talons to kill or dig up graves, and a mouthful of tyrannosaurus-like teeth."

"So, Rose was innocent of the second set of cattle mutilations and the corpse snatching."

"Quite right. I regret that this whole thing resulted in our losing her trust. She didn't take much of her new-found wealth with her, only the perfume and the Victoria's Secret items. I wonder what she plans."

"I don't wish to think about it. I just hope she is well and keeps out of trouble."

"Oh, in case you haven't noticed, the pixies are gone. With two deaths and the ruins the monster left, they've departed to find a more peaceful location."

"I noticed. The garden isn't doing as well, and my knees hurt again."

"We have given out the story vandals damaged the garden, and you fell and broke your arm chasing them off."

"I guess that will have to do. Now if you could only advise me on how to get rid of Clara. If that woman with her chicken soup and weak tea comes one more time to feed me and fluff my pillows, I will go crazy. Isn't there some charge you could arrest me on and lock me up away from her machinations?"

The sheriff rose and entered the rectory. A long cackle of demonic laughter echoed in the hallway as he walked to the front door.

Dennis Maulsby is a retired bank president living in Ames, Iowa with his wife Ruth, a retired legal secretary, and his dog Charlie, a retired CIA operative. A son and grandson live in the Pacific Northwest. His poems and short stories have appeared in numerous literary journals and anthologies, including *The North American Review*, *Mainstreet Rag*, *The Hawai'i Pacific Review*, *The Briarcliff Review* (Pushcart nomination), and on National Public Radio's *Themes & Variations*. Some of his poems have been set to classical music and may be heard at his website: www.dennismaulsby.com.

His Vietnam War poetry book, *Remembering Willie*, won silver medal book awards from two national veterans' organizations. His book of poetry, *Near Death/Near Life*, and a book of short stories, *Free Fire Zone*, both published by Prolific Press, won a gold medal and a silver medal respectively from the Military Writers of America. Maulsby is a past president (2012 – 2014) of the Iowa Poetry Association.

Made in the USA
Columbia, SC
27 December 2019